T. M. DELANEY

Eerie 2

A Collection of 10 Chilling Tales

Copyright © 2021 by T. M. Delaney

All rights reserved. No part of this publication may be reproduced, stored or transmitted in any form or by any means, electronic, mechanical, photocopying, recording, scanning, or otherwise without written permission from the publisher. It is illegal to copy this book, post it to a website, or distribute it by any other means without permission.

This novel is entirely a work of fiction. The names, characters and incidents portrayed in it are the work of the author's imagination. Any resemblance to actual persons, living or dead, events or localities is entirely coincidental.

T. M. Delaney asserts the moral right to be identified as the author of this work.

T. M. Delaney has no responsibility for the persistence or accuracy of URLs for external or third-party Internet Websites referred to in this publication and does not guarantee that any content on such Websites is, or will remain, accurate or appropriate.

Designations used by companies to distinguish their products are often claimed as trademarks. All brand names and product names used in this book and on its cover are trade names, service marks, trademarks and registered trademarks of their respective owners. The publishers and the book are not associated with any product or vendor mentioned in this book. None of the companies referenced within the book have endorsed the book.

Cover photo by Zoltan Tasi on Unsplash.
Cover font from sinisterfonts.com

First edition

This book was professionally typeset on Reedsy.
Find out more at reedsy.com

To everyone who loves a good scare.
Thank you for reading my book.

Also, to my very good friend, Sarah, who always listens, always encourages, always makes time for me, and never judges. I'm so grateful for your friendship!

Contents

Want Some Ice Cream?	1
Man's Best Friend	9
Grotesque	17
Family Business	27
The Beldame	35
Knock, Knock, Knock	42
Into the Woods	48
Apathy	58
Mannequin	66
Identity	80
About the Author	92
Also by T. M. Delaney	94

Want Some Ice Cream?

Jake blinked sluggishly as he slowly woke up. His head felt strange, and though he wasn't fully awake, he had a vague sense of wrongness. It took several more seconds for his brain to catch up with the feeling: he wasn't in his bed. That in and of itself wasn't alarming. He often partied hard, so it wasn't unheard of that he'd wake up on a friend's couch or floor, or even sometimes in a friend's bed. Usually, though, his friends' accommodations didn't poke him in the back so much. And they weren't usually so cold. He groaned and squirmed, trying to get more comfortable. The sound of gravel scraping filled his ears and startled his mind into clarity significantly faster.

He opened his eyes with a snap and took in the sight of a bridge overpass above him. He gasped and sat up quickly, gravel cascading from his hair and down his back, and he grimaced and clutched his head. The world swam sickeningly. Jake looked around nervously as he was overtaken with the creeping realization that he didn't know where he was, much less how he got there. For that matter, he couldn't even remember the date or day of the week. Wednesday? Sunday? He truly didn't know.

Jake pushed himself to his feet on shaky legs and wobbled a few steps until he could lean up against the middle support of the bridge over his head. He looked around the surrounding scenery, trying to see if he recognized where he was. He was dismayed, though, to find that everything was just gravel and grass. The area beneath the bridge could barely qualify as a road, little more than a gravel-dirt path slightly wider than the width of a single car. It seemed he was well outside of city limits, and he couldn't figure out why. He didn't know anyone who lived out in the boonies, so why would he have come all this way out for some kind of party? And why was he alone? No matter how drunk they might have gotten, none of his friends would have ever just left him behind anywhere, much less unconscious outside in the middle of nowhere. Jake shivered, looking around again. He hated being alone.

Except, he *wasn't* alone. A shrill metallic chime to his right startled him and drew his attention. Jake looked down the road and jumped when he saw who…what?…was watching him. It was a man, or appeared to be, who was dressed like a very old-school hobo clown. His clothes were patched and raggedy, and his face was painted into an exaggerated frown that was accented even further by the severe downturn of his lips. He stared ceaselessly at Jake as he perched atop an old bicycle that had some kind of small wagon attached to the back. Just as Jake began to wonder if he were some kind of statue that couldn't move, the clown man raised his hand in a jaunty wave that clashed appallingly with his frown, and he resumed riding his bike, pedaling on up toward Jake.

Jake looked around again, mildly alarmed by the clown's approach. He'd never been a big fan of clowns, especially older style clowns, unsettled by their heavily painted faces that seemed designed to hide secrets. He was also still alarmed that he couldn't figure out where he was or how he'd gotten there.

He didn't want to run, though, like some kind of chicken, so he stood and waited for the clown to get closer. Things did not improve, however, when the clown finally pulled up alongside him. He just rode up, stopped moving, then began staring again, that brutal frown still marring his face.

"Uh, hello?" Jake tried.

The clown ignored him and hopped off the bike to pat the top of a cooler that he was hauling in the wagon. "Want some ice cream?" he asked in a dreary voice that matched his haggard appearance, but not the joy that ice cream should be. Granted, ice cream from a weirdo hobo-clown was more of a nightmare than joy anyway, Jake supposed.

Caught off guard by the question, Jake looked at the worn-down cooler on the even rougher wagon. In extremely faded letters were the words *Jeremiah Bob's Gourmet Ice Cream*. "Oh... no, thank you," he said carefully. "Where am I?" he asked, looking around himself again as if any new clues about his whereabouts might have appeared.

The clown—Jeremiah Bob?—didn't answer the question. Instead, he patted the ice cream cooler again, sad frown still pulling at his face.

Okay, clearly this man was not firing on all cylinders. Jake slowly backed away and shook his head. "No, thanks. I'm gonna go." He continued backing up until there was a good distance between him and the clown before he turned around and began walking away.

"Ice cream!" the clown behind him yelled, beginning to sound angry.

The sound of gravel slowly crunching as the clown began pedaling the bike again was alarming in Jake's ears. He increased his walking speed and cut across the scrubby grass to move from the road he and the clown were on to climb up to the road that the bridge ran along. Hopefully the steeper terrain and his dogged pace would clue Mr. Clown into backing off already. After cresting the edge of the hill to the upper road, Jake paused to look over his shoulder. Down at the edge of the road, the clown still sat astride his bike, staring intently at him.

"Want some ice cream?" he hollered up again.

Jake shook his head and turned to keep walking away. He didn't want *anything* from that creepy man. After a few more quick glances over his shoulder to ensure he wasn't being followed, he pulled his cell phone out of his back pocket to try and determine what the hell was going on. He scanned through his texts first and found that his friend Jordan had invited him and a few others to a party. What was alarming, though, was that instead of an address for the party, there was only a series of GPS coordinates. None of the surrounding details gave any additional clues for what that location was. He tried putting the coordinates into a search engine, but wherever he was had zero cell service, so he couldn't use the internet. He tried calling a couple of people, but there was no signal to accommodate that either. Finally, he settled on writing a text message to Jordan, hoping that as he walked, he would finally wander into the range of a cell tower and that the text would send once service was restored.

Jake put the phone back into his pocket as he followed the winding road before him. He had no idea what would have possessed him to decide to go to a party based on the coordinates alone. Sure, Jordan was a good friend, but this was really sketchy. And it was extremely concerning that he still had no memory of anything from the night or two before waking up below the underpass. The surroundings were eerie too. Why was there no one around? No houses, no businesses, no passing traffic. Just how far out into the country had he gone? For that matter, where was his car? How had he even gotten out there? Had he taken a ride with a friend? But then where were they and their cars? Why would they have left him?

The path before him led into a small grove of trees, and he was relieved for the shade they provided. The sun was high in the sky, and each minute that passed, he became more and more aware of just how thirsty he was. His relief shriveled up immediately as he heard another chime from a bike bell up ahead. He looked down the path and was dismayed to see the same hobo clown from earlier pedaling his bicycle out from between the trees onto the path before him. How he'd gotten around him to show up in front of him, Jake had no idea. He stopped in the path, unwilling to close the distance between himself and the clown.

The clown grinned a sickening grin, completely incongruous with the frowning face paint over the top of his mouth. "Want some ice cream?" he asked again.

Jake bristled. "I already told you 'no'!" he hollered back. He looked to the side, considering trying to cut through the trees to get away from the clown.

"Your friends wanted ice cream."

Jake looked back to the clown in shock. "What? What do you know about my friends?"

The clown mimicked holding a cell phone. "See for yourself." He resumed riding, cutting into the thick trees on the opposite side of the road that he'd come from.

"Hey, wait!" Jake screamed, all thoughts of safety vanishing as he rushed forward. Impossibly, though, the clown had disappeared already into the trees, though Jake could faintly hear him laughing in the distance. "What the heck?" His stomach twisted uncomfortably as anxiety overtook him. Who was that clown, and how did he know his friends? Had he hurt them? Jake remembered the clown's pantomime of a cell phone and hurriedly pulled his phone back out. His photo gallery! Why hadn't he thought of that before?!

He did indeed have photos of the party, but they raised more questions than they answered. They'd all been taken inside a house, but it was a house he'd never seen before and had no idea where to find. Most of the photos showed them smiling and hanging on each other, beer bottles in hand, as though they'd been having a fun time getting wasted. Jake didn't *feel* like he'd gotten overly drunk, though, despite his failing memory; there was no hangover to speak of. Maybe he drank less than his friends? Even more uniquely ominous, each of his friends in one of their photos was seen holding an ice cream cone in their hands. What was with the ice cream? And what was with the freaky clown? The last photo showed them all posed together, arms over each others' necks. Lurking off to the side was the same clown who'd been harassing him since he'd woken up.

Jake needed to find that clown again, frightening as he was. He was the only one so far who had any connection to his missing friends, probably the only one who could tell him where they were as well as where *he* was. But how would he find him? Should he try to run into the trees in the direction he saw the clown go? Or would that just get him more lost than he already was? Maybe if he continued along the road, it would come out around the wooded area and he might run into the clown again? But what if he kept going and then never ran into him? But then again, maybe the clown was dangerous and Jake should instead focus on finding help, like the police? He stared all around, not certain at all what he should do. Then ever so faintly, he heard the chiming bell from the clown's bike again, but it was coming from the trees to the right, the complete opposite direction from where the clown had left just a moment ago!

Shivers crept through Jake's body. "That doesn't make any sense," he muttered to himself. The bell chimed again. Everything within him screamed that this was dangerous and that he shouldn't follow the sound, but he couldn't shake the fear that something had happened to his friends. What if there was a clock ticking? What if he kept wasting time looking for help where there was none to be found, and they all died or got seriously hurt? He heard the bell chime a third time. Gathering all his courage, Jake took a steadying breath and then stepped into the trees, trying to follow the intermittent chimes of the bell.

He stumbled through the tightly packed trees for ages, sharp branches bruising his arms as they jabbed him. How could the clown have ridden his bike through all of this? Profusely sweating and covered in leaves and sticks, he finally found his way to a small clearing. The hobo clown was waiting for him in the center, the characteristically forlorn face staring back at him once again. The hair on the back of his neck stood up at the sight. Everything in him wailed that this was *wrong*, but he didn't know what else to do but seek answers from this clown. There was no one else around, and he still had no cell service. He was out of options. Cautiously, but with an air of confidence that he didn't fully feel, Jake walked across the clearing to the clown.

"I saw the pictures in my phone," he said when he was close enough to not have to shout. "Where is the house this party was at. And more importantly, where are my friends?"

The clown replied, "Want some ice cream?"

Rage burst through Jake. "I already told you that I don't want any of your fucking ice cream! Where are my friends?!"

The clown once again produced a smile that contrasted with his painted frown. "Friends are near. But first, there must be ice cream." He patted the top of the cooler attached to his bicycle.

It took everything within Jake to keep from lashing out again. This was progress, as much as it also felt like a riddle. "Fine," he spat, "I want some ice cream. Please, just tell me where my friends are."

The clown shuffled around his bike to stand behind the cooler, leaning over it with dramatic flair. "Come closer," he said.

Jake approached with halting footsteps.

"Your friends are right here." He popped the cooler open with a flourish.

Jake leaned over to look in and saw that the cooler was filled with heads, the heads of all his friends, mouths opened in terror, eyes frozen forever in shock. With a cry, Jake lurched back and looked up. The hobo clown looked menacing now, a dark glare so deep that the paint across his face was beginning to crack. He pulled a machete from a deep pocket in his pants, and he lunged forward with a roar, the blade swinging in a deadly arc.

Man's Best Friend

Life for the Johnson family was perfect. They had a beautiful blue house with a white picket fence. Dean Johnson was the loving husband of his wife Nancy, and together they were the proud parents of two children, their older daughter Gail and their younger son Davie. To complete the family was their golden retriever, Sandy. The only tragedy that had struck their family had happened just about a year in the past, when their first dog, a black lab named Luna, had gone missing during a camping trip. Dean and Nancy had been heartbroken, their children utterly devastated. They'd held out hope for a while that someone would find Luna and return her to them, but months had passed, and finally they'd had to face reality and accept that she wasn't ever going to come back. Right around the same time, Sandy suddenly showed up outside their front fence, apparently abandoned and in need of a good home. Not wanting their children to suffer any longer nor wanting them to grow up without the warm, fun presence of a pet, Dean and Nancy had decided to allow Sandy into their home as a new pet, and once again, their family was complete. Nothing could shake them now except….

"Dean! Dean come here, quick!"

Dean hurried over to the living room where his wife stood

looking out the window. "What? What is it, dear?" he asked.

"Is that…is that Luna?" his wife asked, pointing to just outside the fence enclosing their front yard.

"Oh, honey, you know it can't—" Dean began, falling short as his eyes fell on the dog out front. Stark black except for a white patch of fur on the chest in the shape of a crescent moon, which had earned Luna her name. "Oh my…it *is* Luna. But how?"

"What are you guys looking at?" Gail asked as she walked quietly up on them.

"Well, we think Luna might have just come home," her mom replied, trying to figure out how to explain to her children that their dog hadn't died after all. She didn't need to worry, though, because the excitement of a returned dog was enough.

"Really?! Davie, hurry! Luna's back!" Gail yelled, running for the front door. Davie gave an answering whoop and followed closely on his sister's heels, content to follow her lead.

"Wait!" their father called, hurrying to rush after them. After all, it had been so long.

He and Nancy made it to the porch just as the kids got the gate opened, and Luna bounded into the yard, running around and chasing the kids, barking merrily. It was the same tenor of bark they remembered always hearing from her. Nancy had a few tears trickling down her face as she smiled happily. "Oh, Dean, I can't believe she's back after all this time!"

Dean hugged his wife. "It's a miracle she survived at all, much less made it back here. Nothing else can explain it. Just like the miracle of Sandy showing up when we needed her most."

Another bark joined the mix, and Sandy came romping around the house from the backyard to join in the merrymaking. Luna froze at the sound of another dog, turning her attention from the children to track the sound. Her hackles rose as the caught sight of Sandy, and she positioned herself in front of the children, growling menacingly. Sandy growled back, and the two dogs snapped at each other ferociously. Dean and Nancy were alarmed, having never seen such behavior out of either dog before. They hurried into action. Dean approached the two dogs cautiously, trying to diffuse the situation, while Nancy hurried to their children and herded them back up on the porch and into the house.

"What's wrong?" Davie cried. "Why are they fighting?"

"I don't know," Nancy said absently, hurrying to grab two leashes from the hall closet. "The two of you stay in here! I have to go help your father." Nancy hurried back outside, finding her husband talking to both dogs who still barked and growled fiercely at each other. "Dean!" Nancy called, tossing her husband a leash. Sandy was already wearing a collar, so it wouldn't be too difficult for him to get the leash clipped to it. Luna wasn't wearing a collar, so Nancy fashioned the leash she held into a slip-leash with a loop at the end that she could slip over Luna's neck. Together, they moved as one, catching both dogs and struggling to pull them apart, somehow making it through the endeavor with neither of them getting bitten in the process, though Sandy did snap sharply at Dean when she felt his hand slip around her collar.

They both huffed and puffed as they struggled to hold back the dogs, who still strained to get at one another. Dean tugged hard on Sandy. "I'll get her to the backyard," he called to his wife. "We can close the gates that separate the two yards for now." Nancy nodded her agreement and hauled Luna along with her to the other side of the house so that she could shut that gate while her husband got the other. Finally, both dogs were secured in separate yards, and the gates were closed. The dogs found each other again, though, and continued their fight through the gate while Dean and Nancy retreated inside.

Both of their children were upset and crying, so Dean hurried to give them both a quick hug. "Hey, it's okay," he said, trying to look upbeat for their sakes. "They just surprised each other. They'll be friends soon enough." The furious snarling outside did not agree with his words of encouragement, and he grimaced slightly. "You both need to stay inside for the rest of the day," he continued. "Go on upstairs and play for now until it's time for dinner." The two kids sniffled but did as they were bid, retreating upstairs. Dean turned to his wife with wide eyes. "What was *that?*" he asked.

Nancy shook her head and collapsed into a recliner. "I have no idea. I've never seen either of them act like that." She paused as the barking and growling burst into a louder crescendo. "Dean, this is bad. We can't keep both of them when they're like that. They're going to tear each other apart, and they might hurt our kids too."

Dean sat in the chair across from her. "I know, but what are we supposed to do? Which one do we get rid of?"

Nancy frowned, looking at her hands, which were fidgeting nervously in her lap. How would they make such a decision? Luna was their dog first, had been their dog for about four years before she'd vanished, and they'd only had Sandy for about a year. But Sandy was so near and dear to their hearts by this point, whereas Luna had faded into memory. It felt disloyal to get rid of either one of them. "I don't know," Nancy finally said. "Should we ask the kids what they think?"

Dean shook his head. "I don't think we can put a decision like that on them."

They sat in silence a little longer, before Nancy finally spoke up and said, "We have no idea what has happened to Luna in the past year...."

"True," Dean replied, "but we don't know anything about Sandy from before she arrived," he pointed out.

"Yes, but Luna *did* instigate the fight with Sandy...so maybe we should get rid of her?"

Dean looked upset. "I picked her from the litter of puppies all those years ago. Do you remember?" he asked. "She was always so protective...." He sighed and swiped quickly at his eyes. He nodded his head. "Doesn't matter. You're right that we're at a disadvantage not knowing what happened over the last year. I'll take Luna to the animal shelter tomorrow before work."

They got up and cooked dinner together, wincing every time the dogs picked up their fighting again. It was going to be a long night if they had to keep listening to that chaos. In between the fighting, Luna would come to the front door and whimper and whine, scratching frantically at the door. Dean and Nancy felt bad for ignoring her, but after her aggressive display earlier, they couldn't trust her. They did feed Sandy out back, not lingering, though, in case she was still too upset. Dinner for the family was a somber affair as Dean and Nancy tried to explain to their children the decision they'd made. Both kids were upset, neither okay with separating from their long-lost dog who had just returned home.

"Well, would you rather we get rid of Sandy?" their mother finally asked tiredly.

"No!" Davie wailed. "You said they would be friends! I don't want to get rid of them!"

"Neither do I," Gail insisted.

Nancy and Dean made eye contact across the table and nodded at each other. They'd made their decision, and they would stick with it. Their children would recover. For now, they had to be responsible and remove the threat of a dangerous dog. They went about calming their children and getting them settled down for bed as best they could.

~~~

Sometime in the early hours of the morning, Dean and Nancy awoke to a renewed round of ferocious barking, this time accompanied by a dog's pained shrieking as well as screams from their son and daughter.

"The kids!" Nancy screamed, jumping out of bed.

Dean reached the door first, leading the way downstairs and out the front door. Both children cowered on the front steps, Gail clutching her little brother close, her hand bleeding profusely. Out in the yard, Sandy was viciously mauling Luna, tearing her to pieces in a ring of bloody grass. Dean started to head for the dogs, but stopped when he realized Luna was no longer making any sound. She was dead. His hand clutched the porch rail tightly. "What happened?" he asked in shock.

Gail sobbed wordlessly as her mother inspected her hand, severely bitten by one of the dogs, so Davie answered, barely understandable through his tears. "W-we didn't w-want you to take a-away our d-dogs," he hiccupped, "so we tried to get them to be friends." He took a great heaving breath. "But Sandy is *mean!* She bit Gail!" He burst into fresh tears again, clutching at his sister once more.

Sandy did this? Dean thought. He'd assumed Luna had attacked the kids and Sandy was defending them, albeit in a very violent manner. He watched as Sandy looked up as she heard her name, standing proudly over Luna's corpse. She looked menacing, almost as if she were smiling, a distinctly non-canine look to her blood-smeared face. She growled again, lowering her head at him. He went cold. "Nancy," he said, trying to sound calm. "Get the kids inside now." He heard Nancy follow his instructions immediately, but then Sandy lunged forward with a sharp bark. Dean rushed toward her with his own yell, determined to keep Sandy from hurting his family. He cried out in pain as her teeth sank as easily into his arm as a knife through butter, his muscles tearing and tendons snapping as she whipped her head back and forth. Finally, the bones in his arms snapped audibly as well, and Sandy let him go. He staggered back, a gurgling cry coming from him as Sandy immediately grabbed him by the throat, biting hard and shaking her head until his neck was torn up enough to leave him bleeding out on the floor of the porch.

Nancy screamed from inside the house, struggling to get the door closed, but Sandy lunged again, breaking through their old screen door and pushing her way into the house before the main door could be shut. Chaos ensued as the children scrambled to get away, and Nancy grabbed the fire stoker from the stand next to the fireplace, striking Sandy across the head with it several times. Sandy would not be deterred, though, and she got around the stoker, pushing Nancy to the ground and grabbing her by the face. Nancy screamed shrilly as, once again, Sandy shook her head violently, as though Nancy's head was little more than a rabbit she had hunted. Nancy quickly stopped screaming or fighting, and Sandy left her where she lay. Nothing remained of her face. Sandy rounded on the two children.

"Mommy!" Gail cried, frozen to the spot in the corner of the room. She couldn't pull her eyes away from the ruin that had once been her mother, shock freezing her solid. Sandy descended upon her like a demon, leaving nothing of Gail behind but shredded flesh and the echo of a scream.

Davie sobbed and threw open the back door, running for the maple tree all the way in the back corner. He was nearly blind from crying so heavily, and he could barely breath. As he ran, he imagined he heard Sandy right behind him, heard the snapping of her teeth, felt the heat of her breath on his heals, her jaws just waiting to trip him up. But he knew he could climb the tree. If only he could make it in time. Just a few more feet. If only he could make it.

Grotesque

"What the heck is that thing?"

"I dunno. How should I know?"

"Well it's on top of your store."

"Yeah, but I didn't put it there. Some dumb kids must be pulling some kind of prank."

"It's so weird, though. I wonder who put it there. And why? And just what is it?"

"Some kinda gargoyle, I think? Like on cathedrals?"

"It's a grotesque," Mira said unexpectedly, startling the group of adults she'd quietly joined on the sidewalk. The little eight-year-old craned her head far back to look at the stone statue that had mysteriously appeared on top of the general store in their small, isolated town.

The store owner peered down at her. "A what?"

Mira blinked slowly at him. "Gargoyles are drain spouts," she said. "Grotesques are just statues." She had learned that distinction when researching the cathedral that had appeared in an animated movie she'd seen once. Mira loved learning new things. She was very smart for her age, which other kids hated, and some adults did too. She also knew that she was just a little off, just a little peculiar in her behavior, which was what made adults shy away from her. Sometimes she tried to fit in better, compared her behavior to others' to try to fit in. She didn't like how the ostracization made her feel; she wanted to be treated like everyone else.

"Uh huh…" another of the lingering adults said. He smirked a little, like he thought she was making things up, which was ridiculous. Mira never told lies; she was a good girl. "Whatever you say, sweetheart," the man said patronizingly. "Why don't you just hurry along to school now. Mr. Calloway and I gotta see about getting that thing off of there."

Mira let herself be pushed along down the sidewalk, and with one last look over her shoulder at the statue, she headed along to school. All the kids at the school were chattering about the grotesque, though most of them incorrectly referred to it as a gargoyle. Even the adults were in on the gossip, though they tried to hide it from the children, all of them wondering who Mr. Calloway had upset enough to pull such an intricate prank on him. It really was a mystery, but, Mira thought, not something so simple as a prank.

~~~

The next day when Mira arrived at school, she found a minor hubbub happening there as well. A grotesque had appeared on top of her building too, the building that housed kindergarten through seventh grade. The neighboring building for eight through twelfth grade did not have any such statue. She listened to pieces of conversations around her. The reigning theory was that it was a senior prank, though it really was far too early in the year for their shenanigans to start acting up. Mira didn't understand the idea of senior pranks, or really just the idea of causing mischief and harm in general. It seemed like it would be better just to be nice to everyone and not cause trouble. Her mother always praised her for following instructions. Maybe the older that people got, the less praise they received, so the ornerier they became?

Mira pushed her way past the bigger kids to get a better look at the newly appeared grotesque high above on the school. It was as hideous as they usually were, this one complete with a pig snout, vicious looking teeth, horns, and wings like a bat's. Still, a warm feeling filled Mira at the sight. She wanted to be closer to it. She looked up at the sky again and frowned at the sight of oddly thick, roiling clouds. It was a few weeks before summer storms would start kicking in. And there was something about those clouds....

"Mira!" a sharp voice called out.

Mira jumped, her eyes landing on her teacher, Ms. Weatherspoon, who stood next to the rest of the class. They were all lined up in two even rows, waiting for her to join so they could head inside to the classroom. Mira hurried to run over, blanching under her teacher's annoyed frown. She hated for anyone to be cross with her. Hated it, but also knew that she would be finding a way to get on the roof during the school day, maybe at recess. Rules were important, but everything within her said to go and see the grotesque sooner rather than later. Her mother said to follow the rules, but she also told her to trust her gut. Mira was a good girl who listened to her mother.

~~~

At recess, Mira snuck away from the rest of the kids and the teachers who monitored them and made her way for the fire escape along the far side of the building. It ran all the way to the roof, so it was no trouble for her to make it up. She crossed the roof and came to a stop beside the grotesque. It was even more hideous up close and personal, but in a cute kind of way. Mira contemplated it for a moment, then smiled. "I'm going to call you Chester," she said, patting it on the snout. "Is that okay?" Chester didn't reply, but she felt like surely he approved of the name. Distantly, Mira heard the teachers blowing their whistles to signal that recess was over. "I have to go now, Chester, but I'll come see you again soon!" Mira grinned as she hopped down the fire escape stairs. She had plans soon! Plans to meet someone! Even if only a statue. For a young child with few friends, it was exciting indeed.

~~~

A few mornings later, Mira eyed the swirling clouds above again. Though the heavy, unnatural clouds had persisted for days, there had been no rain. The non-stop cloudy sky was unusual, but Mira shrugged. It didn't seem like something she needed to be concerned about. There were a lot of people buzzing around town this morning as she walked to school. Over the past several days, since the very first grotesque had appeared on the general store, dozens more had cropped up unexpectedly around town, baffling all the adults. No matter how much gossip spread about who might have done it and why, no conclusive evidence could be found. It was as though they'd literally sprung up from nowhere, though they all assured one another that of course that couldn't possibly be the case.

They fretted about the swirling clouds in the sky as well. The weather must be doing something to interrupt cell signals because no one could get a call out to anyone outside their region to check on the weather. Internet connections were down as well, a typical hazard of a location like their town. Theirs was a remote town that was very difficult to travel to and from; the roads in and out were all rutted and washboarded, as liable to pop a tire or break an axle as get you anywhere, and there were no other towns for miles through the surrounding wilderness, so they couldn't go elsewhere to find communication. They were effectively cut off from the world, and some of the adults were getting nervous.

"If we're so isolated, then how is anyone coming to put up these gargoyles?"

"Stupid, it's because it's someone who lives in this town."

"But then where did they get the statues?"

"Um…well…maybe they made them themselves?"

"Right. And where do you expect they got the stone from, huh? There's no quarry anywhere near here!"

"I don't care where they came from. I'm telling you, they're some kind of omen. We shouldn't keep them here. We need to take them down!"

"Don't be ridiculous. Besides, we haven't figured out how to get them unstuck yet.

Mira ignored it all, making her way to school like usual. Today, though, she wasn't going to go straight to class. The teachers had been watching all the students closely since the grotesques had begun appearing, as though they thought staring steadily at the children would reveal the culprit. They also weren't allowing outdoor recess anymore since the weather was so suspicious, so she hadn't been able to visit Chester since the first day. She missed him. So few of the other kids wanted to be her friend because she was "so weird," so he was kind of the only friend she had.

When she got up to the roof, though, she found a small group of other children already crowded around him, mostly kids older than her. The ringleader, a bully named Josh who was two years older than her, strutted around in front of Chester, showing off.

"Look at this dumb thing," he said. "None of the adults in this stinking town have figured out how to get rid of these ugly things, but you know what I think? I think they're just scared of them. I think they're afraid to touch them. And I bet all of you are too!" he yelled, pointing his finger accusingly. "Well *I'm* not scared." He reached out and placed a finger mockingly on the statue's head.

Mira puffed up angrily. She didn't like it when people touched her without permission, so surely Chester wouldn't like it either. "Stop that!" she yelled as she marched over to the other kids. "You leave Chester alone!"

The kids all guffawed. *"Chester?!"* Josh exclaimed incredulously. "Leave it to a freak like you to come up with such a dopey name. And don't you tell me what to do," he said, poking her hard in the chest. "I'm bigger than you, so I can do whatever I want. I can even *break* him." He reached out to a friend who was holding a baseball bat. "Give me that!" he demanded.

"No!" Mira cried, but one of his flunkies held her back.

Josh hauled back and swung the bat down with all his might. It crashed into Chester's head, and his ear broke off with a loud crack. Instead of celebrating, though, Josh clamped his hand to his own ear with a scream. When he pulled it away, blood covered his palm. Wide-eyed, he stared at it and staggered backwards in shock, toppling over the edge of the building at the last minute. The rest of the kids screamed and rushed forward to see what had happened, the flunky letting Mira go in his hurry. Upon seeing Josh splayed out and bleeding on the ground below, they all raced off to scatter before they were found and questioned by teachers.

Mira stayed behind, though, sniffling and coming forward to check on Chester. She gently picked up his ear that lay on the ground and then patted where it was supposed to be. "I'm sorry, Chester," she wailed. "I couldn't stop them. But I'll fix it! I'll bring glue tomorrow and put it back where it goes." After the encounter with the kids that morning, Mira couldn't bear the thought of sitting in class all day, so instead, she just curled up beneath Chester's broad chest, her arms wrapped around his forearm, and she snuggled with him.

~~~

The next morning, she slipped into her mother's garage and pocketed a bottle of super glue, placing it in her jacket pocket next to Chester's ear before heading out the door, waving goodbye as her mother hollered at her from the kitchen to be careful on her way to school.

As she neared the center of town, Mira glanced up at the sky, and her jaw fell open. High up in the sky, dipping in and out of the roiling clouds, several large winged creatures flew. They didn't look like birds, though. More like some kind of flying reptiles, something that certainly shouldn't be up there. All the store owners were out in the street in a panic, all pointing and shouting.

"What are they? What do they want?"

"How would anyone know that, you dolt? Don't ask stupid questions."

"Those gargoyles were omens! I *told* you. They're bringing

us misfortune."

"No," Mira replied calmly. "That's not right at all. Gargoyles and grotesques are meant to protect a building by scaring away demons."

Again, all the adults eyed her in bemusement. "Child, get out of here," one of them said wearily. "We're getting ready to try a new method for removing them. We can't risk waiting any longer."

"But—" Mira was cut off before she could speak further.

"Woo! Go Mr. Calloway!" one of the younger store owners called, watching the wiry old man climb onto the roof. Mr. Calloway began hacking away at the statue with a machete, gasping as with each hit, blood starting to stain his shirt from within.

One of the adults in the crowd gasped. "Mr. Calloway, stop!"

"I told you, they're *ominous villains!*"

"We've gotta hurry and get them down somehow. I have a bad feeling!"

Mira turned away in disgust—people were always in such a rush to destroy anything different!—and hurried for school. Once again, she made her way up to the roof. "Good morning, Chester!" she called as she approached. She pulled the super glue from her pocket. "Ta da! I brought the glue as promised!" She quickly sat about applying the glue to Chester's ear, her tongue poking through her lips in concentration. After getting the glue applied, she carefully aligned the ear again and got it placed where it should be. "There! Good as new now." She leaned against his back, weary again as she thought about what was happening in the town. "The adults are trying to get rid of all the others like you, and they're getting hurt for it. They don't understand that you're here to help." She glanced up at the sky again. "You're here because of them, aren't you?" she asked. "You knew they were coming."

As if on cue, the figures in the sky above moved in formation and dove for the town below. Screams and shouts carried all the way to the school from the town square. As she watched, mildly disinterested (after all, she wasn't the one in trouble), a couple of the flying figures broke off and headed for the school. Seeing them up close, the only word that Mira could apply to them was "demon"; they looked like evil incarnate, all scaly black and leathering wings, red eyes, and gleaming sharp teeth. The building shuddered and shook as one crashed through the side of the building, the other doing the same at the neighboring school building. Mira watched, alarmed, as several students were thrown from the building, landing in bloody heaps all over the school grounds.

She turned quickly to Chester. "Aren't you supposed to be protecting us? Can't you help them?"

Shockingly, Chester actually moved this time. He pointed at the students suffering below and also pointed toward the town center, then shook his head, pointing at his ear. Next, he pointed at his ear again, pointed to Mira, and nodded yes as he pointed at the glue bottle still in her hands.

"The others rejected you. But you'll help me because I helped you?" she asked quietly, and Chester nodded again.

One of the demons flew up level with the building and charged at Mira. Chester sprang spryly to life then, charging forward and swatting the demon out of the sky deftly with his giant stone fist. Then he turned around, tucked Mira into the crook of his arm, and took off flying into the air. He flew away from the school, away from the town center, flying over the small neighborhood that Mira lived in.

Mira gasped as she saw the roof of her house in shambles. "Chester, my mommy! Help my mommy!"

Chester just shook his head and kept going.

Mira sobbed as she watched her house get smaller and smaller. "Mommy! Nooo! I want my mommy!" She clasped her hands over her eyes and wept bitterly. Her heart broke again, not for the first time in her life, as she was once again isolated. Why couldn't she just be like other people? Why couldn't she just be normal? Why did she always have to be alone?

Family Business

Peter Rasmussen looked like a harmless, unassuming, nerdy pencil pusher, and he knew it. He used it to his advantage. It made him the perfect door-to-door salesman. When he showed up on someone's front doorstep, all cheery smiled and bespectacled, toting along his briefcase with "the highest quality set of encyclopedias money could buy," none of the simple, frilly housewives he encountered would hesitate to let him into their homes to show them his wares, not one of them concerned that their husbands were far away from home. No one looked twice at him. No one feared his intentions or that he might be dangerous to them. That's what made him the perfect thief and killer.

He eyed the house before him, small and yellow with quaint little white shutters on the windows, lacy curtains hanging on the inside. A couple of toys littered the front yard. Children were good; children were leverage to use if the mother got brave. The father, he already knew, wasn't at home; he'd watched him leave for work that morning. Watched him leave after kissing his family goodbye, the perfect family man, leaving jauntily for work, not knowing he would return home a widower. Peter grinned maliciously and walked up to the front door, giving it a peppy knock. When the door opened, he put on his best smile. "Hello, there, ma'am! My name is Peter Rasmussen, and I'd like to talk to you about this lovely set of encyclopedias that I have to sell." He held up his briefcase and gave it a pat. "May I borrow a moment of your time?"

The woman who'd answered the door eyed him a little more shrewdly than most of the housewives he encountered, and for a moment, he thought this was a lost cause. His worries proved unfounded, though, when her face broken into a smile and she opened the door more widely. "Why of course, young man," she said, allowing him through the door. "Encyclopedias, you said?"

"Yes, ma'am!" Peter boomed. As he passed through the door, his eyes immediately began taking stock of the items in the living room, assessing what might be of most value. "I saw your children's toys outside and thought you might be a prime candidate to purchase a set. They'll really help with their education!"

"Oh, what a fine idea," the woman simpered. "They should have a look too, then. Kids!" she hollered up the stairs to her right. Two children, a boy and a girl around the age of twelve, appeared at the top of the stairs. "Kids, this is Peter Rasmussen. He wants to talk to us about buying some encyclopedias!"

She spoke as if this were the most exciting thing to happen all day. For a simple housewife, it probably was, Peter mused darkly.

"Well, come along!" the woman encouraged, clapping her hands lightly. "Come down and meet the nice young man." The children wordlessly exchanged a look with each other, and then with their mom again, who nodded encouragement.

What a couple of little weirdos, Peter thought to himself. All the same, he kept his smile wide. "Hello there, sport!" he said to the boy. "And you as well, little lady!" he added to the girl, giving a ridiculous little bow. He knew how to schmooze when he needed to.

"Hello," they said in union. They were eerily similar. Twins perhaps?

"This is Daniel and Delilah," the woman said. "Oh, and I'm Mrs. Sanders," she added with a giggle. "Please, have a seat and show us these lovely encyclopedias!" She gestured to the living room.

Peter took a seat and got right into his spiel, having uttered it so many times he didn't have to pay it any mind as he rattled it off. Though they had been used several times now, the encyclopedias were still in pristine condition. They were his way in, his way of setting his victims at ease, so he had to take great care of them. The woman sat listening, nodding occasionally, but her attention was more on her two children than on him.

"Have you always been a salesman?" the little boy asked as he finished his spiel.

"Yep! Bit of a family business," Peter answered, thinking back fondly on his father who had showed him the trade, though he had added he own embellishment on it as he'd gotten older.

"We have a family business too," Daniel said.

"Ah, going to be a chip off the ol' block, are ya?" Peter asked. He was getting tired of humoring the kids, but his opening would appear soon enough. He just had to be patient.

"Me too!" Delilah exclaimed. "I'm going into the family business too."

Peter raised an eyebrow. Whoever heard of a little girl aspiring to business. She was supposed to be planning to marry and have a family of her own. It was only right, for goodness' sake. "Ah, you mean you'll marry and bring your husband into the fold, of course," he said, giving her a patronizing look.

Delilah's face darkened. "No, I don't need a husband to—"

"Delilah!" her mother called sharply. When the girl turned to her mother with a pout, her mother sternly shook her head. "Mind yourself," she said with a meaningful look. The girl huffed, but complied, and Mrs. Sanders returned her attention to Peter. "So, do you have anything else to show us, Mr. Rasmussen?"

Ah, and his moment had arrived at last. "Actually, ma'am," he said as he reached into his jacket, "it's your turn to show me something." He pulled a revolver from the inside pocket of his jacket and pointed it at the two kids. "Your jewelry, any money, and anything else of value. I want you to bring it here, right now, or your children are dead."

Mrs. Sanders' face fell. "Oh! Oh how could you...please, don't hurt my children!"

Peter smiled cruelly. "Do as I say, and your children will be fine," he lied. "Now hurry up!" She wiped away an errant tear and hurried from the room, apparently anxious to comply. *Too easy,* Peter thought to himself. He turned his attention to the kids while waiting for their mother to return, and he was surprised to find them both looking very calm, their faces almost blank as they regarded him. They really were *weirdos*. What kind of kids weren't afraid to have a gun turned on them?

The mother returned, carrying nothing but an old wooden chair. It looked like it was worth a few pennies at best. Peter stood in surprise. "What on earth is this?" he demanded. "I said to bring things of value!" Before he could say anything else, a painful slice cut across his wrist and made him drop his revolver, while another painful slice came across the back of his ankle, severing his Achilles tendon with a snap. He screamed and collapsed in pain. "What the hell?" he bellowed.

The children passed into his vision, each holding a knife. Delilah paused to pick up the gun, and she expertly emptied the bullets before setting the gun aside well out of his reach. She turned to her mother. "How was that, Mom?" she asked.

Her mother smiled encouragingly. "Very good, dear. You too, Daniel! However, both of you need to practice more on faking emotion. Normal children would have been afraid of his gun. You must remember to play the role correctly," she lectured, pointing sternly with her finger. "Otherwise, you run the risk of your victim figuring out what's going on before you've gotten them." She frowned as Peter spat a curse at her as he struggled to get back to his feet, her face turning cold. "That's quite enough out of you, Mr. Rasmussen. You won't be needing to speak anymore." She passed a cloth to Daniel. "You know what to do, sweetheart."

Daniel folded up the cloth and approached Peter. Peter struggled as best he could, but Delilah came up behind him and grabbed two fistfuls of hair to help keep him still as Daniel forced the gag into his mouth and tied it off. Peter continued trying to scream, but it was too muffled now to be heard outside the room.

"Perfect!" Mrs. Sanders said with a gleeful clap. "Alright, you know the next steps! Just as your father and I have shown you. Do well, and your father will have nothing but praise for you!"

Peter's eyes widened in fear as the two children turned as one and smiled down on him cruelly. Together, with only a little help from their mother, they manhandled him into the chair the woman had brought into the room, and they tied his arms and legs to it, completely immobilizing him.

Their mother came around inspecting each knot of rope, nodding in satisfaction at each one. "Perfection. Your father is going to be so surprised! Why don't the two of you come help me get supper ready now?"

"Aw, Mom," Daniel whined. "Can't we have a little fun before Dad comes home?"

"Yeah," Delilah agreed. "Haven't we earned it?"

Mrs. Sanders smiled indulgently at her children and ruffled their hair. "Oh, alright, but only a little. Don't get carried away just yet!" She turned and left the room, humming under her breath as she began cooking dinner. She smiled a little when she heard Peter's muffled screams resume as her children had their fun.

~~~

Mr. Sanders sighed as he entered the kitchen from the garage. "What an awful day," he complained to his wife as he took his coat off and sat his briefcase on the floor.

"Aw, my poor dear husband," Mrs. Sanders replied, wrapping her arms around him in a hug as she kissed him in greeting. "What was it today?"

"Ugh, those meat-head managers wouldn't know a good idea if it bit them on the nose," he sighed. "It feels like I'll never make any headway at that company."

Mrs. Sanders rubbed his shoulders. "I'm sorry, sweetheart," she consoled. "But at least it's the weekend. *And*, your children have a surprise for you that I just know you're going to love. Want to see it?"

Mr. Sanders smiled at her. "Before that delicious smelling dinner you've been cooking?"

"Oh, I think it's worth waiting on dinner just a bit. It'll give us a lot to talk about while we eat!" She pushed him playfully toward the living room.

"Alright, alright!" Mr. Sanders said as he laughed. "Kids!" he called. "Your mother says you have a surprise for me!"

The children came running, grinning from ear to ear. "Yes, come on!" they exclaimed, each taking him by a hand and tugging him the rest of the way.

Mr. Sanders eyes widened as he took in the sight before him. A young man sat trussed up to a chair, his shirt ripped open to reveal oozing, bloody cuts all up and down his belly and chest. A gag was stuffed in his mouth, and tear tracks stained his face. He looked up at Mr. Sanders with fearful, pleading eyes. Mr. Sanders looked away from him and crouched before his children. "Did you do this?" he asked seriously. When they nodded, he added, "All by yourselves?"

"There was very little assistance from me," their mother confirmed from the side of the room.

Mr. Sanders got up and approached the young man, stalking around him slowly as he inspected the ropes, ignoring the young man's flinch as he ran a hand over his chest to inspect the cuts.

"Not too deep!" Delilah chirped.

"Yeah," Daniel added, "because he'll last longer and be more fun if we're patient!"

Mr. Sanders finished his inspection of their victim and crouched before them again. "I am *so proud* of both of you!" he exclaimed, pulling them both into a big hug. "I just *knew* the family business would be carried on well by the both of you!" He stood, taking one of their hands in each of his, laughing as he realized he was spreading their victim's blood everywhere. "Whoops!" he said jovially. "Let's wash up, and then we can sit down to your mother's lovely dinner, and you can tell me all about how you snared your prey! And," he added conspiratorially, "we can make our next plans for him! After all, he'll last for several days, easily. We have to make sure we get our fill of fun before he's done."

The Beldame

Benny sat in his car at the corner of the street, staring at the bank across the intersection. He drummed his fingers on one hand anxiously on the steering wheel. His other hand was clutched around the stab wound in his side. He couldn't believe his gang had turned on him. Trying to tell him that *he* was a loose cannon, that *he* had gone too far? He was the leader of their little gang of bandits, dammit! How dare they tell him that he was anything? They were supposed to listen to him and jump the moment he told them too. Ungrateful little bastards; they were only as prosperous as they were because of the leadership that he had provided. And to turn on him the way they did…he gripped the steering wheel in rage. He was lucky he'd heard the hammer cocking on the gun when they'd tried to shoot him in the back and had been able to dodge at the last minute. It had been pandemonium after that, bullets and curses flying. He'd fired back, and he knew that he'd killed one for sure, maybe a couple. In the end, it was his own little brother, Ricky, who had been the one to slash his side open. But he had paid for his betrayal with a point blank .44 magnum round to the forehead. Benny didn't feel an ounce of remorse; Ricky should have known better than anyone not to cross him. He was his right-hand man by nepotism; he shouldn't have let anyone cross him, much less have joined in the mutiny himself.

Benny leaned back in the seat of his car with a sigh. He was lucky he'd been able to get out of there and into his car before it was too late, and he'd managed to lose any pursuers in the city traffic. But now he was out in some backwards, no-name town in the middle of the country with very few options. He'd have to get money before he could really do anything else. After that, he'd have to start from scratch and build a new crew, he guessed. Find better people to work with than the last bunch of screw-ups, definitely a group that would follow instructions better, who would know to never question him, no matter what he decided to do. He was the leader! If he wanted to murder someone, it was his right. If he wanted to torture someone, do unspeakable things to them, it was his right! His last crew had whined at him to just stick with smaller crime to avoid racking up greater offenses against them if they were caught, but that was chicken shit! The point was to *not* get caught. There was no fun to be had in simple thievery; he wanted to have some excitement too.

But to start, he needed money, and he would get it here in this town at their lovely little bank. He drove across the intersection and parked in an open parallel parking spot right in front of it, perfect for his quick getaway. It was early afternoon on a weekday, so there were fewer people around: easier for managing the hit with no one to back him up. He walked through the front door and took in all the details. Three customers in the lobby, two tellers behind the counter, no security guard on watch—all women. Nothing but a bunch of backwoods simpletons. Perfect. "Everyone freeze! This is a holdup!" Benny screamed.

The three customers jumped in surprise and stared in shock

at the gun in his hand. Likewise, the two tellers both jumped and instinctively held their hands up in the air. "Please, don't hurt us," one of them said.

"Shut up!" Benny yelled with a dark glare. "The three of you, on the ground!" he barked at the customers. The three of them lowered themselves to the ground, though the woman closest to him, instead of looking afraid, had a smirk on her face, as though to say, *You just made the biggest mistake of your life.* "Eyes down!" he yelled, not appreciating the defiant attitude.

He turned back to the tellers. "You know the drill, start bagging up the money. And if either of you hit any alarms, silent or otherwise, you're dead." The two tellers complied, slowly starting to place money into a couple of bags they procured from behind the counter. Benny waved the gun impatiently. "C'mon, hurry up! Some of us have lives and places to be!" He eyed the closed vault to his left. "And don't forget in there," he said with a jerk of his head. "I want whatever is in there too."

One of the tellers looked at him incredulously. "Um, that's not a good idea, sir," she said quietly.

Benny narrowed his eyes and leaned in menacingly. "I didn't ask your opinion. Now open that vault."

The teller hesitated again. "But—"

She screamed and dropped to the ground as Benny shot her in the arm. He pointed his gun at the second teller. "Do you want to argue, or do you want to do as you're told?" he asked coldly.

The teller, a very young and attractive girl, raised her hands in the air. "Whatever you say, dude." She didn't look scared, though. Almost thrilled. Maybe she was into violence? Benny let his eyes trail up and down her form as he watched her move to the vault. He'd have to consider recruiting her, depending on her attitude. Maybe she wanted out of this no-name town, desperate enough to follow any order he gave her. The idea thrilled him.

He had to abandon his filthy thoughts as soon as the door to the fault opened, though, because a chilling cackle immediately filled the air, coming from everywhere and nowhere all at once. "What? What the…what is that?" he exclaimed, turning frantically in all directions as he tried to find the source.

"You're done for," said a voice to his right. It was the customer who'd smirked at him earlier. She waived her hand to get the two other women to stand with her, and they backed up into a corner, their eyes fixed on him.

"No one told you to get up!" Benny shrieked, struggling to keep his voice under control. "Back on the ground, right now!"

The woman just shook her head. "Nope. We want to see this."

"It's sure to be amazing," the young teller agreed. When Benny turned, he found her standing as well, her arms wrapped around the other teller he'd shot, supporting her. She shook her head. "You certainly have it coming, mister," she said.

He sneered at them all. "What are you going on about? Hurry up and get me my money so I can get out of this hellhole!"

The cackling filled the air again. *Get him 'his money' he says. Just who does he think he is? Little worm, taking what surely isn't his to take.* A chilling, echoing voice filled the air.

"Who is doing that?" Benny cried again, his voice cracking as he looked all around himself.

Imbecilic little man, the voice crooned again, sounding like it was coming right into his ear, *tangling with The Beldame.*

Benny jumped. "The Bel what? What kind of freak are you, bitch?"

Killed his baby brother, he did. Killed many many people. The voice moved around him as it spoke before moving close into his ear again. *Killed many a soul he pulled in too close. Too many dirty secrets to hide. Too many skeletons in the closet. Skeletons with names that make him feel...things.*

Benny jumped again, real panic in his eyes now. "You...how do you..." His face hardened. "You don't know anything!" He yelled belligerently. "Certainly can't prove nothin' to no one! Now, if you're not going to bother showing in person, cut the spooky shit, give me the money, and get the hell out of my way!" He headed for the counter to collect the money bags the girls had been filling.

Aren't you worried about that wound of yours? It festers as foully as your mouth and soul.

Before he could ask what that was supposed to mean, the wound in his side zinged him with a sharp pain, and then it felt as though it was beginning to writhe. Alarmed, he struggled out of his shirt and ripped the bandage aside. He couldn't contain his screams at the sight. Hundreds of maggots were crawling through the wound, some falling loose and tumbling down his leg to the floor. "Argh!" he screamed again, swiping frantically at the wound, ignoring the searing pain in favor of cleansing the wound. No matter how many he knocked loose, though, several more took their place, as though they were rapidly growing from within him. He spun in a frenzy then, tears in his eyes as he looked all around. "Show yourself!" he cried.

The air before him shimmered, and a woman faded into view. She was impossibly tall, shrouded in a long dark cloak, wild red hair curling around her face and cascading down her back. *"Here I am,"* she said, her voice still echoing eerily all around the room. *"What now, that you can lay your eyes on The Beldame?"*

Benny narrowed his eyes. "Now you die!" He raised his gun

and fired. The bullet appeared to just vanish, the air before the woman shimmering briefly again. Then the gun in his hand blazed up red, instantly burning his hand as it began to melt, turning into a puddle of molten metal where he dropped it at his feet. He stared in horror first at the destroyed gun, then up at the witch—for that was surely what she must have been—who watched him with a calculated gaze.

"You have no ability to kill me," she said smugly.

Without another word, Benny turned and ran for the door, crying out when he crashed into it and found it inexplicably locked. He also realized that the room had fallen dark, the afternoon sunshine outside somehow failing to pass through the windows into the bank. "Let me go!" Benny screamed, pushing hard on the door.

"After you have the gall to attempt to steal my own wealth and that of my coven? And threaten the people of this town, who have been under my protection now for centuries? I think not."

An invisible force slammed into Benny, throwing him into a wall and pinning him there. "No! Please, please, let me go! I'm sorry!" He struggled again to no avail. "You made your point!"

The woman shook her head, a haughty expression on her face. *"The point is hardly made, for you are a dull-witted fool who will learn nothing. And your hubris now leaves you at the mercy of my diablerie."*

Agonized screams tore from Benny again as his body began to contort and contract, slowly molding into new forms.

"What oh what should you be?" The Beldame mused, shifting Benny from one animal to another: a dog, a pig, a fish, a bird, a worm. No matter the form, Benny always stayed cognizant, completely aware of who he was and what was happening to him. Finally, The Beldame settled on a cockroach, placing a jar

over him and deftly capturing him before sealing the jar with a lid full of small holes to allow the passage of air. She stared at him with a dark glee. *"You shall live a long life indeed, always in whatever form I deem fit, for however long I deem fit, and you will only find death when I deem it time."* Her smile widened as the cockroach seemed to shiver.

She looked back up at the room around her, meeting the gaze of the newest daughter in her coven—proud to see her using her talents to heal her wounded coworker. Then she shifted her gaze to the other women of the room, women whose families had been under her protection for countless generations. They all nod respectfully, showing their gratitude. With a wave of her hand, she closed and sealed her vault again before vanishing in a shimmering mist, the room brightening again in the wake of her departure.

Knock, Knock, Knock

Kelly grinned with glee as she listened to the merry sound of popcorn popping away in her microwave. She'd survived the too-long work week and had made it to Friday, and it was finally time to have some fun! With spooky season fast approaching, she'd been longing to start watching nothing but horror films. She'd chosen a good one to stream tonight too, a rare movie she'd had to find on a probably illegal website. It was an old movie, one she'd never heard of until recently while she was scanning online forums looking for recommendations. She'd seen so many horror films that it was getting harder and harder to find any that she hadn't seen yet.

This one, though, according to the people she'd found discussing it, was supposedly cursed. She smirked, laughing as she fondly thought back to middle school when *The Ring* had come out and everyone at her school had been whispering about how *that* movie was cursed, one girl going so far as to say she'd gotten the "seven days" phone call after watching it and doubling down on the prank by skipping school on the seventh day. The people in the forum that Kelly had found were taking the supposed curse surprisingly seriously, so much that she wondered if they were really a bunch of kids rather than the adults their profiles said they were. None of them had watched the film, all claiming anecdotal evidence that bad things happened to the people who watched it. Kelly shrugged her shoulders, dumping her bag of popcorn into a bowl and carrying it to her living room. Some people just couldn't handle spooks. She was old hat at it, though. Very little scared her anymore.

She turned all her lights off, got settled in, then started the movie. It started oddly enough, no opening credits, not even any opening studio logos. Maybe those had been removed by the host site? That would be pretty dangerous, though, as far as copyright law was concerned. Kelly shrugged again. Didn't matter; it certainly wasn't her head on the line if the streaming site was breaking the law. Slowly the movie played on, and she focused intently. It was one of the oddest films she'd seen in a long time, very abstract, with little in the way of plot, as far as she could tell. There were barely any people in it so far, and those who were present had yet to speak. There wasn't even a score, though there was ambient sound. *Just how old is this movie,* she wondered. She knew older movies were different in style, but this different to the extreme. She tilted her head, an appraising look on her face. It had promise, but she wasn't sure if she would be impressed come the end.

About fifteen minutes in, she was startled by a knock at her door. She frowned. There shouldn't be anyone visiting her so late at night. None of her friends were available to hang out that night, and she didn't know any of her neighbors. All her lights were out, and the movie wasn't turned up that loud, so she decided to just ignore it and pretend she wasn't at home. There was no sound beyond the movie audio for a few minutes, but then the knocking came again. She was getting annoyed.

All she wanted to do was relax that evening, and instead she had people causing her trouble. She still tried to ignore the knock, but it kept coming intermittently.

Knock, knock, knock. Knock, knock, knock.

Finally, with an irritated groan, she paused the movie and got up. The knocking had her so distracted that she'd lost track of what was happening in the movie and would need to rewind it, not that there was anything particularly eventful going on. It was mostly creepy imagery. She walked quietly to her door and peered through the peephole to see who was knocking. But there was no one there. She sighed in annoyance. It was probably a group of teenage punks running around the neighborhood playing pranks. She hoped someone would catch them soon and read them the riot act.

Kelly turned to head back to the living room, but the knocking came again.

Knock, knock, knock.

She spun quickly and hurried to the peephole, determined to catch them this time. Once again, though, she couldn't see anyone there, not right outside the door, nor further off in her yard. An uneasy feeling settled within her. Surely they couldn't run that fast. No, she thought, shaking her head. More likely they were ducking to either side of the door where they knew she couldn't see them through the peephole. She strained her ears to see if she could hear any movement, but the world outside was as silent as the grave.

She looked at the windows, thinking. She'd closed all the blinds before getting started with the movie since night had fallen and it was getting dark outside. It was nice to know that the kids outside couldn't see her but also scary that she, in turn, couldn't see them to know what was going on. As she pondered the windows and door, the knock happened once more. She pursed her lips, and with great effort, she returned to her living room. She had no idea why they were choosing to pester her tonight—it wasn't like she was some kind of neighborhood menace; she barely talked to her neighbors—but she refused to let them ruin her evening. She would just go back to watching her movie, turning up the volume if she had to.

She clicked backward along the progress bar a few minutes, trying to find where she'd started getting distracted. It all seemed to jumble together, and she sighed again. Everyone swore by this movie, so she didn't want to not finish it, but the abstract nature of it was frustrating her. Behind her, she could hear the knocking start up again. Not only was she being harassed, but she was probably watching a bomb too. She continued watching the film, ignoring the occasional knocking from the front door. She made it perhaps another ten minutes into the film before loud knocking on the window across the room nearly caused her to fall from her chair as she jumped in fright.

KNOCK, KNOCK, KNOCK!

Okay, enough was enough. She was calling the police. She fumbled around, looking for her phone. The darkness in her house, lit only by the dim light from her computer screen, felt strangely oppressive, and she longed to turn some lights on. Lights inside, though, would only confirm for whomever was outside that she really was home, and they would give them a view of her silhouette to see where she was, neither of which appealed to her. The loud knocking on the glass sounded again, making her jump. For the first time, she wondered if it wasn't a group of kids. What if it was someone who truly meant her harm?

Heart pounding now, she finally succeeded in finding her phone. She pulled up her dial pad, but then hesitated before dialing 9-1-1. She was scared, yes, but did this really constitute an emergency? She didn't really know what was going on… maybe she shouldn't tie up the emergency line. When the sound didn't happen again immediately, she pulled up the internet on her phone and looked up the phone number for the local police station, electing to call them instead. When the call was answered, she paced around her home, trying to explain what the issue was. "Uh, hi. Um, there are kids, or someone, outside my house making a lot of racket."

"Mmmhmmm," replied the bored-sounding police officer on the other end of the line.

"I'm scared to go out and say anything to them. Can you please send someone over?"

"You said they're just knocking on your door?"

"Yes. Well, and my window. They won't go away." She could almost hear the disgusted look she felt like the officer must be giving the phone. Now that she was trying to explain this all, she felt like a fool, especially because the knock still hadn't occurred again. They'd probably finally decided to leave right as she made this call.

The officer sighed. "What's the address?" After Kelly answered, the officer continued. "I'll see if we can get someone to do a drive-by in your neighborhood eventually, but it won't be soon. We've got a lot going on tonight. Goodbye." The officer hung up without preamble.

Kelly stared at her phone. The town she lived in wasn't that big; what on earth could be so busy that they couldn't take her more seriously? As she debated whether to return to the movie or give it up as a lost cause, it happened again.

KNOCK, KNOCK, KNOCK! KNOCK, KNOCK, KNOCK!

Kelly jumped a mile as the loud knocking came simultaneously from both the window and the door this time, and she started to cry. Why wouldn't they just leave her alone? The knocks became incessant, barely stopping for a moment. She stumbled back into the living room, intent on turning off the movie, but her computer appeared frozen, though the movie continued to play (hadn't she paused it?). The images were abstract as ever, but dark and threatening, and the ambient noise had been replaced by a chilling, haunting score. The knocks repeated even louder, and Kelly shrieked in terror, fleeing from the room and leaping up the stairs two at a time. She ducked into her room and into the closet, slamming the door and bracing it with shaking hands. She sobbed raggedly, trying to get her breathing under control.

Downstairs, she could hear the thundering knocks, could almost feel the vibrations running through the planks of wood beneath her. It sounded as though they were moving all around the house now. How could her neighbors not hear what was going on? Finally, the knocks stopped again, and the house fell eerily quiet. She sat frozen in the closet, too terrified to so much as twitch.

KNOCK, KNOCK, KNOCK!

The pounding came from the wall directly behind her. Kelly lurched to her feet with a strangled cry, wrenched the door open, and threw herself through the threshold, directly into a hulking shadowy mass of claws, and teeth, and bones. Her eyes widened as it took her, leaving naught but the fading echoes of a chilling cry.

Into the Woods

Vicki took deep breaths as she jogged through the quiet forest, soaking up the sharp, tangy smell of pine. She loved these early morning jogs, just her and no one else in the world but her friend Wendy, who could just manage to keep up well enough to not hold back her pace. They always chose this particular trail because it was one of the more rugged in the state park near their homes. With the difficulty of the terrain, few people ventured onto the path, especially early in the morning on a Saturday. Vicki loved it, though, loved the burn in her legs and her lungs as she pushed her body's endurance, and Wendy apparently concurred since she joined her almost every Saturday. They kept good company, each providing a modicum of safety to the other, but both also knowing well how to maintain easy silence to give the other the space they needed. They flourished from not having to see and interact with other people. This was their opportunity for meditation, to sort out their minds and the stresses of the previous week before charging into the next.

The isolation from other people also meant that they saw more wildlife on their runs, the animals not having been scared off by other individuals. They frequently saw all kinds of birds, chipmunks, squirrels, and marmots, silently pointing them out to each other as they jogged. Sometimes they were lucky enough to see elk, moose, foxes, and coyotes. "Oooh," Wendy said that morning around panting breaths, "look, a fox!"

Vicki smiled as she saw the little red-haired canine watching them from the safety of a rocky ledge hanging over the trail. It was so cute!

"What are we gonna do it we run into something bigger out here, like a bear or cougar?" Wendy huffed as she jogged.

"Eh," Vicki replied, "I think we're too close to civilization for them to be any issue here." She grinned conspiratorially at Wendy. "Besides, I have less to worry about than you do."

"Huh?" Wendy gasped, looking her way.

"I'm much faster than you, so I can outrun you to safety!"

Wendy stuck her tongue out. "Rude! I'd never leave you behind!"

Vicki laughed. "Which is why you're the guaranteed victim while I'll make it home at the end of the day!"

They carried on with their jog for a while longer before Vicki frowned a little as they crested a small hill. "Do you hear that, Wendy?" she asked. She kept hearing an odd clicking sound that she was unused to hearing.

"Hear what?" Wendy wheezed, struggling to keep up.

Vicki huffed in annoyance. "That clicking sound." She paused, giving Wendy time to try and hear it.

"Ah yeah," she finally said. "What is that?"

Vicki frowned again. "It's the beginning of summer; maybe it's cicadas starting to come back?"

Wendy glanced over at her, looking unconvinced. "That doesn't sound like any cicadas I've heard before…."

Vicki shrugged and tried to push the sound from her ears as she continued jogging, but it persisted, getting louder and louder. Somehow, the forest around them almost started to feel darker. To her right, suddenly, she caught a flash of movement in her peripheral vision. She chanced a glance to her right as she ran but couldn't see anything through the dense trees and undergrowth. "Wendy, did you see that?"

Wendy looked wide-eyed now and pale too. "I thought I saw something running in the trees," she said quietly. She instinctively pulled away from the tree line, crowding into Vicki's space.

"Ah! Watch it, Wendy!" Vicki exclaimed as she tried to keep from getting hit by Wendy's pumping arms while also trying not to trip off the path. "Move over!"

The path looped into a small clearing, and they both came to a stumbling stop at the sight before them. A body lay on the ground. A dead body so damaged by decay that they could barely make out any discernible features beyond that the body was clearly human. "What on earth?" Vicki exclaimed. She leaned a little closer. "This body doesn't really look like it's rotting from being dead for a long time," she said. "It's almost as though it's been eaten away at by some kind of substance. Maybe acid?"

Wendy stared at the body too, looking green in the face. "What could have done this?" she asked fearfully. She jumped as the clicking rapidly grew louder and faster. "What *is* that?!" she yelped.

Vicki looked all around, trying and failing to find the source of the sound. "Maybe whatever did this?" she asked, pointing at the body. They both locked eyes and turned as one to run, taking the path in the closest direction to the parking lot. Vicki pumped her arms and powered forward. Only her regular conditioning and training kept her from panicking and blowing all her energy and breath too soon. She was built for endurance. She could get away from…whatever that was, and she would be okay.

"Vicki! Vicki, wait! Please!"

Vicki looked over her shoulder and saw that Wendy was falling behind. She had never been as strong an athlete as Vicki, not as motivated and driven, not as physically capable. Suddenly Vicki's jokes of leaving her behind to an attacking predator had become a stark possibility. She hesitated slightly, slowing her run to a choppy jog. "Wendy, hurry up!" she hissed, reaching back a hand as though she could somehow will Wendy to move faster.

"I'm trying," Wendy sobbed, clutching at a stitch in her side as she tried to catch up.

Distracted by watching Wendy and with her form shot all to pieces, Vicki neglected to pay attention to the trail conditions. A large gnarled root growing over part of the trail caught her toe. She reeled wildly off balance and shrieked as she fell to her left, tumbling down a steep slope. Brambles and roots and branches tore at her skin and clothes as she fell, sparking additional pain through her body. She hit the bottom hard with a gasp that blew all the air from her lungs.

"Vicki!" Wendy screamed from above.

Vicki lay dazed on the ground and watched as Wendy looked down at where she'd fallen, bit her lip as they locked eyes, then turned and continued running.

Vicki's heart clenched. "Wendy!" she struggled to scream as she summoned air back into her lungs. "Wendy, no! Don't leave me here!" But Wendy was gone. Vicki couldn't believe it; despite all her jokes, she would never have really left Wendy behind. At least, she didn't think so….

Vicki looked around wildly, trying desperately to figure out what to do. She was too far from the trail and down too steep a slope to make her way back to it. Plus, she vaguely thought she might still hear the weird clicking up that way, though it was hard to tell with the adrenaline coursing through her making her ears roar. She would have to find her way back to the parking lot from where she'd landed. Terror coiled in her chest. She wasn't experienced with path finding, and there was some*thing* out in those woods following them. She would just have to hope that whatever it was chose to continue pursuing Wendy rather than herself; she shuddered at the grim thought. After looking around carefully to ensure she was alone, she pulled her cell phone out, hoping that she would have a signal to call for help. She usually did have a signal up on the crest of the trail, but she cursed as she saw no bars this time, apparently too far out of range of the cell towers down in the ravine.

She climbed to her feet, wincing as the ankle of the foot that had caught on the root twinged. She tested her weight on it. It didn't feel like too bad of a sprain, but running on it was going to hurt terribly. *Whatever,* Vicki thought viciously. *It can hurt tomorrow. Now is not the time.* She pushed onward, finding quickly that running was no longer an option as she struggled through the thick underbrush. She proceeded in the general direction of the trail above her, trying to remember all the upcoming twists and turns. The path generally followed the river that flowed down in the ravine, just a little off to her left. If she followed that, she figured she would eventually find her way back to the trail or the parking lot. She kept her ears open as she hiked. She didn't hear the creepy clicking sound anymore, but the woods were eerily quiet, no other animal sounds to be heard. Even the leaves were quiet with no wind to disturb them. It was unnatural and unsettling.

Vicki pushed onward, moving as fast as the thick undergrowth and her injured ankle would allow her. She tried to keep as quiet as she could, both to not draw attention and to try and hear if anything began pursuing her again. At one point, she heard faint screaming off in the distance, and her stomach dropped. Was it Wendy? Had the thing gotten her? A few minutes later, and she started thinking she could hear the clicking, faint but getting closer. She fought valiantly to control the panic trying to overtake her, knowing that it would only cause her harm in the long run. She had to keep a straight head. She followed the base of the ridge line, walking straight and slightly left as it kept pushing her closer and closer to the river.

"No, no!" she moaned, coming to a stop on the damp earth that she walked along. She'd reached a dead-end. The path had veered directly to the river, which continued on in front of her. It was too wide and rough at this point to cross, but she hated the idea of doubling back far enough to try and cross it, not after she'd come so far. She clenched her fists, trying hard not to cry. She studied the river. Could she survive trying to swim in it? It or one of its tributaries would eventually flow near the parking lot. The trick would be navigating once she was in the fast-moving water. And not drowning.

Loud clicking resumed above her, and she looked overhead. There, high on the ridge line was something. Something big that she couldn't quite make out, but it looked *wrong*. Leaves along the steep slope trickled down towards her as it moved forward, and Vicki shrieked. Without further thought, she flung herself carelessly into the river, knowing instinctively that she stood a better change surviving the raging water than she did surviving an encounter with whatever that thing was.

The water consumed her quickly, dragging her under and covering her head. She struggled hard against the rapid current, fighting with all she had to pull her head above water. Finally she broke free, choking and gasping for air and trying to blink the water from her eyes so that she could see. The rapids roared all around her ears, so deafening she could hear nothing else. She bit back a yelp as her leg glanced off of a submerged boulder, adding another layer of injury. Up ahead was a fork in the river, and she swam hard for the right, believing it was the path that went nearer the parking lot. She made it, and blessedly, the waters began to calm, this side a smaller branch off the main river.

Ahead of her was the ruins of a tall mine shaft, the primary draw for visitors to the state park. Very little of it could be explored internally anymore due to instability, but the mine was very much a part of the region's history, so it was still of interest to tourists. It was also a popular location for field trips during the school year. The teachers had to keep a close eye on the children, though, because there were old mine shafts everywhere within the park, just the right kind of draw for curious, fearless youths. The sight of the primary mine shaft rallied hope within her. It was only about a quarter mile from the parking lot. The trail should be just ahead. She could make it! Vicki hauled herself out of the river and started staggering through the woods again up to the asphalt path she could see before her. She'd barely reached it and started walking when a haggard voice called out to her.

"V-Vicki!"

Vicki jumped and looked to her right. "Wendy!" she cried. Wendy was laying just off the path between two trees, blood pouring from her left shoulder where her arm used to be attached. Vicki's hands trembled before her, unsure what to do. "Wendy, what the—"

"It took my arm," Wendy moaned. "It grabbed me. I thought I was dead, but it ripped off my arm. That's how I got away, because it took my arm," she continued babbling, clearly in shock.

"C'mon," Vicki said, grabbing her none too gently and dragging her to her feet. "We have to go!" Wendy whined and whimpered as Vicki roughly jostled her over to the path, but they didn't have time to waste. They had to hurry before that thing came back!

As if on cue, the clicking resumed once again, much louder than it had earlier. This time, it was accompanied by the slithering sound of leaves being walked through. Vicki slowly turned her head toward the sound, terrified what she would see. There, just on the edge of the path, right where she'd just picked up Wendy, stood some kind of *monster*. She stared at it uncomprehendingly, her mind refusing to understand what her eyes were seeing. It must have been nearly eight feet tall, and it looked like some kind of insect-lizard hybrid. Large, sharp pincers near its mouth moved, making that horrid clicking sound. It scuttled forward.

Vicki screamed loudly and shoved Wendy at it without hesitation, trying and failing to block out her screams of pain and betrayal as the monster crunched her within its pincers. Vicki turned and ran. Maybe it would stay focused on Wendy. Maybe she could still get away! She diverted from the path, knowing that it twisted and turned through the woods, taking a longer route. After all, the quickest way to a destination was a straight line! She could make it. The monster might be fast, but she was fast too! She was equipped to run through rough terrain. She'd trained for it all her adult life! She lived for it, and so she would live! She would get away! She would make it! She—

She stepped and heard the splintering sound of wood, and she crashed through the ground, through rotted, weakened wooden planks long since hidden under a bed of fallen leaves that in turn hid an old abandoned mineshaft. She fell a frighteningly long distance before landing with a ghastly squelching sound. All she felt initially was pain, and she roved her hands over her body trying to take stock of the situation in the dim darkness she'd landed in. She could barely see; only the tiny radius of space around her was lit, barely, from the opening far above her. The skin along her side rippled alarmingly, and she found that she'd landed with a plank of wood stabbed through her ribcage into her chest. From her seriously pained breathing, she wondered if it had gone so far as to puncture her lung. Her ankle throbbed worse, too, and she feared that this time it was well and truly broken.

She dropped her head back in despair. How would she get out of this? Even if there was some sort of ladder, she was in no condition to climb out now. She'd just have to wait and hope that someone came near enough to hear her call for help. Far to her left, she heard several small, delicate clicking sounds. "Help!" she screamed as best she could with one compromised lung. "Please! Is there anyone up there! I need help!"

To the side, several smaller versions of the monster walked into the dim light. *Babies,* she thought. More of them approached from the right. *I landed in a nest.* "Help," she croaked as the first ones reached her and began pincering her limbs. "Ow!" She felt the burn of acid dripping from their pincers, just as she'd seen evidence on that corpse before. A bigger one approached her head and started gnawing at her nose. Vicki screamed and screamed as they began to slowly eat her, the acid and slicing pincers burning through her. "Please, help!" she wailed despairingly. But help wasn't coming. It was early on a Saturday morning, when people rarely came, just as she liked it, just as she always planned for.

Apathy

Tyler stared dubiously at the man in the Easter Bunny costume who waved at him from far across the stark field. At seven-years-old, he considered himself far wiser than his little five-year-old sister, who's hand he grasped tightly as she struggled against him.

"Tyler, let go of me!" Katie whined. "I wanna go meet the Easter Bunny!"

Tyler watched as the bunny man gestured for them to follow him into the woods. "That's not the Easter Bunny," he said, and he turned away, dragging Katie along behind him. Katie fought and screamed at first before turning sullen, pouting pathetically as he towed her along behind him, heading back home from school. When they finally got home, Tyler set about the typical pattern he'd established since Katie had started school that year, going straight to the kitchen to get them each a snack to eat while they sat down to work on their homework. It was simplest this way, because he could easily turn to see what Katie was working on and help her as needed. There was no one to help him, but that was okay, because he was pretty smart. No one else in second grade had figured out advanced subtraction as fast as he had!

Over in the living room, their father would snore away

in front of the TV, resting up before the big fight he would inevitably have with their mother when she came home from work, angry to find him being lazy. His snores drowned out the TV, which was always on one of those boring channels where everything was in black and white. Tyler hated all of those shows, full of happy families who spent every day together, the mom at home tending the house and kids, the father coming home from work every day with a big grin and a pat on the head for each of his kids. Those shows told lies, and Tyler didn't like liars. If he and Katie were really lucky, their parents' fight would continue on upstairs for a while, and they would be able to watch a few cartoons together. It was also a matter of luck whether either of their parents would put something together for dinner; if they didn't, Tyler at least had long-since become adept at microwaving chicken nuggets.

While he and Katie were finishing up their homework, their mother came home. Surprisingly, she carried a box of pizza with her and an actual smile rather than a scowl. "Hey, kids!" she said, plopping the pizza box over the top of their homework papers.

"Hi, Mom," Tyler replied, hearing Katie echo him as he carefully extricated their homework from beneath the pizza before it got ruined by grease. He tucked it all away into their backpacks so he could put those by the door, ready and waiting for the next school day.

"Today was a good day," his mom said, bustling around to fix herself one of her "grown up" drinks that the kids weren't allowed to taste. There were a lot of "grown up" things in the house that he and Katie weren't allowed to see or taste or touch. Tyler thought it was terribly unfair that they didn't in turn get any "kids" things that were off limits to their parents. "We sold a really big order, so Mr. Jones gave me a bonus!" she said cheerily. She looked slyly over at the living room. "Let's just keep that a secret between us, though, m'kay? Your dad doesn't need to know about that. That can just be Mommy's money."

Tyler just nodded mechanically as he got a piece of pizza onto a paper plate for Katie before getting one for himself, already anticipating the fight that would happen between his parents when Katie inevitably said something. She was too young to know better, which his mother was certainly old enough to know. He couldn't understand the way her mind worked. "Katie and I saw a weird man in a bunny costume today," he said, looking up to see if his mother would listen.

"Mmhmm, that's nice," she said, pulling out her phone to read something on the screen. "Oooh, there's a sale at the department store in the next town this weekend! I can get some new shoes!"

"He was really weird. He wanted us to follow him into the woods," he tried again.

"*I* wanted to see him, but Tyler wouldn't let me talk to the Easter Bunny," Katie pouted.

Their mom looked over at them with a frown. "What? Tyler, what kind of stories are you filling her head with now? Don't be telling her foolish stuff like Santa Claus and the Easter Bunny being real."

Katie looked up tearfully. "Mommy, that's mean. You sound just like those big kids at school! I *know* the Easter Bunny is real. I *saw* him, and I'll get to talk to him one day!"

Her mom wearily waved her off and carried off half of the pizza to her bedroom upstairs. Tyler sighed and gave Katie a one-armed hug to stop her tears while he ate his pizza with the other hand, making a mental note to try and find out who the kids bullying her were. After they finished their food, they crept past their father who was still passed out in the living room, several cans of beer precariously balanced around him, and Tyler got them a bath before reading Katie a story to put her to sleep. Finally, he fell into his own bed, completely exhausted.

~~~

The next morning, the bunny man approached them from a different location. This time, he was lurking under the small country bridge they had to cross on their way to school. He gestured enthusiastically, trying to coax them down to the shadows below.

"Tyler, *please!*" Katie begged. "Let's go see him!"

Tyler eyed the man as he dutifully pulled Katie along. He didn't understand why she was so eager to talk to him. The costume he was wearing looked as if it had been bright pink once, but it was a gross dingy brown now, and the fur was starting to matte in some places and thin in others. It looked as if it smelled too. Tyler wrinkled his nose. "We don't have time," he finally said. "We have to go to school."

"I hate school," Katie said, pulling against his hand and kicking a rock viciously. "All the kids are mean to me. No one wants to be my friend."

Tyler sighed and led her up the steps with the other kids entering the elementary school. "I'll talk to your teacher when school's over," he said. "Maybe she can help."

Katie looked unconvinced, but let him steer her to her classroom before he changed directions and hurried down the hall to his classroom before he got marked tardy again.

~~~

By the time the school day ended, Tyler had barely spoken to anyone. He'd thought about asking some of the other kids if they'd seen the bunny man, but he was afraid they'd make fun of him if they hadn't, and he didn't want to alienate himself even further than he already was; they already looked down on him for his shabby clothes and thrift store tennis shoes that were full of holes. He hadn't even considered telling his teacher, Mr. Kenny, because he'd made it abundantly clear from the first day of class that he didn't like Tyler. Tyler didn't fully understand it, but it was somehow related to something that happened between his dad and Mr. Kenny's wife. He didn't understand why that should have anything to do with him, but maybe that was just a difference in being an adult.

Katie was the one who spotted the bunny man before he did that day on the way home from school, Tyler too lost in thought. This time, the bunny man was standing directly on the side of the road, almost close enough to reach out and grab them as they passed. He also held a basket over his arm, waving once again with his free hand.

"Oooh, Tyler, he has Easter Eggs! C'mon, let's talk to him! Maybe we can get Easter Eggs this year!"

Tyler held her arm firmly, groaning in exasperation. Was it even Easter yet? It didn't seem like it was quite time. Not that it mattered. He knew without a doubt that the bunny man wasn't the Easter Bunny. Why couldn't his sister understand that? "Katie!" he finally yelled sharply, making her jump. He so rarely raised his voice at her. "Stop being so stupid!" He deftly pulled her around the bunny man, glaring as he passed. "He's not the Easter Bunny! The Easter Bunny isn't real! We don't get Easter Eggs because our parents don't love us!" He fought back angry tears that threatened to fall, a painfully hard task when faced with his sister's crestfallen expression.

When they made it home, she ran away from him up to their room, slamming the door behind her. He sighed, knowing he would have to make it up to her later. For the meantime, he followed his normal routine and sat down to his homework. All the pages seemed to swim together before his eyes, though. What did any of it matter? What was the point? Who even cared? He was just so tired.

He was still staring at the unfinished homework when his mom came home from work, much closer to her usual sullen demeanor than she had been the day before. There was no pizza today, and she went straight to making one of her drinks, this one twice as tall as usual. Tyler took a deep breath, bracing himself to try telling her about the bunny man one more time. "Mom, that weird bunny man was waiting for us before and after school again today."

His mom held up a hand, downing half her drink in one gulp. "What are you talking about, Tyler?" she asked, resting the glass against her temple.

Tyler sighed. "There was a weird man in a bunny suit yesterday who waved to us. He tried to get us to follow him today too...." he trailed off.

His mom was leaning around the doorway, glaring into the living room. "Lazy oaf," she muttered, finished the rest of her drink. "I work all day, and he just sits on his butt. Doesn't even take care of the house. How exactly is that fair?" she demanded turning to Tyler.

He shrugged his shoulders, defeated.

"Hey!" his mom shrieked, making him jump, but she wasn't yelling at him. She stomped into the living room. "Get up, you bum!"

The sound of his parents screaming insults at each other followed him as he trudged up the stairs, his homework forgotten. When he walked into the room that he and Katie shared, she glared at him from where she sat perched on her bed before hurrying to slip under the covers, pulling them over her head. "Katie," Tyler said tiredly. "I'm sorry for what I said earlier." She didn't reply. "Katie?" he tried again. When once again she didn't respond, Tyler sighed, switched off the light, and climbed into his own bed. It was still early; they hadn't eaten dinner and hadn't bathed or brushed their teeth, but what did it matter? Neither of their parents would notice, and Tyler was just so weary of it all.

~~~

"Tyler! Tyler, wake up! He's here! The Easter Bunny is in our backyard!"

Tyler groaned and blinked his eyes open sleepily. It was almost 8:30, well past the point that they should have left for school, but he couldn't bring himself to care. His whole body jostled as Katie shook his arm impatiently again. Apparently she'd forgotten that she'd been mad at him the day before.

"Tyler," she whined. "He's out there, right by the creek. Let's hurry and go say hi!"

She trotted out of the room, and Tyler made himself get up and follow her downstairs to the kitchen. She was standing by the back door when he arrived, eagerly bouncing on her toes and pointing. He looked through the window on the door and saw the bunny man waving at them from the tree line just past the boundaries of their backyard. "Katie," he said, "I really don't think…." She glared at him, stopping him short.

"Fine," she said, sticking her chest out. "I'll go meet him by myself. I'm a big girl. *I'm* not scared." She pushed the door open and scampered through, hurrying across the yard.

Tyler thought about grabbing her arm to stop her again, but he let her go. She wanted to see him, so let her see him. He turned away to pour himself a bowl of cereal. As he sat down with it, his mom entered the kitchen, yawning widely. She did a double-take when she saw him.

"What are you doing here?" she asked him surprised. "You should be at school already!" She looked around a little. "Where's your sister?"

Tyler ate a spoonful of cereal. "She went out to see the bunny man."

"What?" their mom replied. "Bunny man?" She looked through the window over the sink.

"She thinks he's the Easter Bunny. He called her into the woods." Distantly, he started hearing screams. They were faint, but they sounded like Katie.

His mom's eyes grew wide. "What? Why didn't you stop her?!" She didn't wait for an answer before racing out the door, screaming Katie's name as she ran.

Tyler shrugged, not looking up from his cereal. *You didn't care,* he thought to himself. *So I don't care.*

Mannequin

Carrie sighed as she jumped for the umpteenth time that morning, her peripheral vision catching on something vaguely threatening, only to realize that it was just a stupid mannequin. Only a few days into this new job in this small department store, and already she was seriously regretting it. She hadn't even wanted a job, but her dad had made her. She was only sixteen! She figured she had the rest of her life ahead of her after college to work, so why should she have to work now? But he'd put his foot down and declared it "time for her to start learning to take care of herself." She'd threatened to disobey; what could he really do? He was legally responsible for providing for her needs, like food and clothing. And then she'd blanched when he threatened to buy her nothing but the cheapest clothes he could find—"say goodbye to all your favorite labels"—and to just stop buying snacks altogether—"those chips and snack cakes aren't a necessity, after all"—and she'd despaired to find herself backed into a corner. And thus, her options were presented to her: retail or fast food. She couldn't bear the thought of working in a hot kitchen for hours on end, so the department store it was.

It wasn't even really that bad a job, in all honesty. She had a good eye for fashion, so she took it upon herself to help customers who came in with questions, guiding certain people away from truly heinous choices and leading others to hidden gems they otherwise might not have seen. She also got an employee discount, so at least her paycheck would be getting more distance for the nice new clothes she wanted for her fall wardrobe; she wanted to start the next school year in style! It was just that the mannequins were so *creepy*. All store mannequins were alarming, but these ones were the worst she'd ever seen. Instead of the plain white plastic that most stores seemed to favor, these came in a wide assortment of actual skin tones—probably in an effort to be more racially inclusive, but in her mind just adding to the eerie uncanniness of the figures. They also had more well-defined facial features than most, though again, blank eyes and frozen faces detracted horribly from the otherwise lightly realistic appearance.

She caught herself staring at one of a small young girl. She'd been posed with her arms up as if she were celebrating or dancing with joy, a perfect fit for the cute sundress she was wearing, but her head was tilted, eyes downcast. She looked irrepressibly sad. Carrie frowned. Was that how she'd been positioned yesterday? The mannequin was reasonably new, which was the other odd thing. According to Carrie's coworkers, the store manager seemed to like to update the mannequins regularly. Ones that had been there for a few months would suddenly vanish and then new ones would show up. None of them knew how he had the budget for such constant turnover of the mannequins, and the bitter running joke was that he could afford it because of how little he paid his employees. Carrie had no experience with such matters, but she was perfectly willing to jump on that bandwagon of dissent, already disgruntled that she had to work in the first place.

And at such early morning hours too! She was the oldest of the newer individuals hired for the summer season—only by a few months, but apparently that was enough—and younger enough than the long-haul staff who had stayed for a while for some godforsaken reason, so she kept getting stuck with opening the department store, the others not interested in having to be up early on summer days, and especially weekends. So there she was, every morning at 9:00 am, getting let in by the manager who went straight to his office to probably do nothing but sit on his butt while she went around the store tidying up, getting all the displays organized and clothes properly refolded, and other such tasks until it was time for the store to open at 10:00. Not long before opening, other employees would arrive to help take care of customers and run the cash registers.

She rounded a corner to take care of the last section, and she screamed a high piercing shriek as one of the mannequins swooped into the aisle in front of her, its hand raised for her face. She stumbled back and fell to the ground, her shock rapidly turning to anger as an obnoxious, guffawing laugh broke out. The mannequin was set back into an idle position, and her most obnoxious, pain in the butt coworker leaned out from behind it, a smug smirk on his face.

"Mike!" she seethed. "What the f—"

"Ah ah ah," he cut in, waggling his finger rudely in her face. "None of that language, missy! You know Mr. Peterson's rules."

Carrie bristled. Who was Mike, only three years her senior and a total head case, to lecture her about her behavior? "Hmph. I'm sure there's a rule out there too about messing with his property! Look, you've nearly broken this one!"

"Oh?" Mike said, eyebrows raised. "Wanna fix him?" He pushed the mannequin so that it leaned towards her and laughed as she jumped away instinctively.

"Stop that!" she insisted, her face beet red.

"Oh, how could I?" he asked with faux innocence. "You're so ridiculously scared of these things, how could I possibly resist pranking you with them?"

Carrie gritted her teeth. Days that she had to work with Mike were the worst. "Just grow up, you jerk," she said as snidely as she could muster before turning on her heel and marching away. All she heard behind her, though, was snickering, and it only made her angrier. It was going to be a long day.

~~~

The rest of the week continued in much the same way. Days where she had to work with Mike were guaranteed to have a least one moment of him startling her with a mannequin. And as if that weren't bad enough, she scared herself plenty with the dumb things every time she noticed them in her peripheral vision. Sometimes, she could even have sworn that they moved as she saw them in the corner of her eye, though of course that was ridiculous, and they were stationary the moment she got her eyes trained on them.

As one week rolled into the next, things got even worse. She didn't know why Mike had gotten such a hangup on pestering her, but he was really upping his game. Now, when she would come in first thing in the morning, some of the mannequins would be in different places than they had been the night before. The first time, she didn't even realize that it must have been Mike's pranking. The little girl mannequin with the sun dress she liked was lying on the floor, face tilted into the floor and arms raised high, almost like a child warding off a blow.

Probably had gotten knocked over by some dumb kids the night before and the store closer hadn't bothered to pick her up. Carrie had steeled herself and made herself pick the girl up, setting her back in place and forcing her limbs and head back the way they were supposed to be. It was surprisingly difficult to do, like the joints weren't properly lubricated or designed.

After that, though, each day, something was off about one of the mannequins. Some were in the aisles, others on the ground, others hovering near doorways, some clustered together in groups, almost as though they were plotting some kind of sinister scheme. Having to constantly wrangle them back to their assigned positions was annoying and also difficult, many of them surprisingly much heavier than she'd thought a mannequin would be.

Four days into dealing with this mess, she was ready to kill Mike. She had no idea how he was doing it either. It was rare that he would work closing shifts, so she didn't know how he could mess up something in the afternoon that the evening staff wouldn't correct before closing. Maybe they were just that lazy? The only other person there as late as or later than store closing was the manager, Mr. Peterson. Carrie had no doubt that *he* would be too lazy to fix a wonky mannequin, instead expecting his staff to do it, but he certainly wasn't the type of man to run around pranking his teenage employee. He hadn't spoken to her beyond the exceptionally brief interview and her first day on the job as he'd passed her off to another employee for training. She didn't even hear from him when scheduling was determined; he just posted a paper schedule to the wall outside his office and expected them to follow it without question.

The last straw came about two weeks after Mike's first prank on her. After getting let into the store by Mr. Peterson, she headed for the break room to put her purse and lunch box away inside her little locker, but she was met with resistance when she tried to open the door. Frowning, she pushed harder, and the door budged maybe half an inch. What on earth? She pulled away and then rushed the door, pushing all her weight into it. It gave enough that she could see into the dimly lit room; it was full of mannequins. She cursed and pushed her way into the room. This was beyond ridiculous! Angrily, she threw her belongings into her locker. Then she backed up and shrieked as she felt fingers scrape over her back. She whipped around, finding one of the mannequins closer than she'd originally thought it was. A creaking sound to her right caught her attention, and she blinked as one of the mannequins seemed to sway slightly. She frowned and edged away from the mannequins and then out the door. She had no idea how Mike had managed to make one move, but she was done with suffering silently. It was past time to report him.

She stalked out of the room and then marched back to Mr. Peterson's office. She knocked heavily on the door, barely waiting until she heard him grunt in reply before pushing her way in. "Mr. Peterson," she said, "I need to talk to you."

He blinked back at her slowly, like he was unaccustomed to having an employee come see him in his office. "What seems to be the problem, uh…." He trailed off.

"Carrie," she said, rolling her eyes. You think the least he could do was remember his employees' names.

"Right, Carrie," he agreed. "What's wrong?"

"Mike has been messing with the mannequins and trying to scare me."

He gave her a look. "What now?"

Carrie sighed. "Mike. He thinks that the mannequins scare

me, so he keeps moving them around the store and trying to startle me with them. There's several of them in the break room right now!"

He gave her a dubious look. "Mike hasn't had a shift all week. He and his family are on vacation."

She was taken aback, though in retrospect, it had been odd that she'd never at least seen him briefly during shift time overlaps. She'd just thought maybe he was trying to avoid her so that she couldn't yell at him. "W-well," she stammered, "there's a whole bunch in the break room right now, so *someone* moved them!"

He gave her another weird look. "Now now, Claire," he said with a condescending tone while getting her name wrong as well, "there's no need to start backpedaling. I can understand if you have a crush on a boy, but there are better ways to go about getting his attention than getting him in trouble."

"I...*what?!*" she exclaimed.

He looked at his watch and grimaced. "Now, I have a lot to take care of today, and you are rapidly running out of time to get this store ready for business, so go on out there and fix any mannequins that you tampered with along the way."

He shooed her with his hand as though she were a cat until she left, completely flabbergasted. Did he seriously think she liked Mike? And that she was lying? She looked back at his door again, but she didn't know what else she could say to try and convince him since he'd apparently already made up his mind. If Mike really was gone, then someone else was messing with her. But why? Just because it seemed like she was a little creeped out by the mannequins? She was hardly the only employee here who thought they were alarming, sometimes even slightly ominous. They certainly felt alarming now, since they were somehow making their way all around the store.

She really didn't want to have to haul them all back out into the store, but there really was no other choice. Not if she didn't want to get fired, and she *really* didn't want the lecture she'd get from her dad if she had to come home with that news. So, she buckled down and headed for the break room. After getting the door opened again, she blinked, taking in the sight. Three mannequins in various poses loomed, seeming to stare back at her. She stared around the room, trying to think. Hadn't there been four a few minutes ago? She shrugged and grabbed the first one to start putting them back, shuddering at the slightly warm temperature of the arm in her hands. It seemed like something fake should be cooler.

After getting the mannequins back in place, she spent the rest of her day distracted, half of her mind on helping customers and talking with coworkers, and the other half on trying to figure out who could be pranking her if it really wasn't Mike. It truly stumped her; none of her other coworkers seemed to have any issue with her. She'd probably pissed off a few customers here or there with her candid commentary about their selections— though really, if they asked her opinion, they shouldn't get mad at her honesty—but none of them would have the ability to pull off moving the mannequins around to the extent that they had, right? The only other suspect she could think of was Mr. Peterson, and she had to snort at the thought. She couldn't so much as imagine him pranking an employee by messing up a few piles of folded clothing, much less hauling mannequins around everywhere. He was too lazy, and if he didn't like someone, he could just fire them.

Finally, it was the end of her shift, and it was time to collect her things to go home. It was the end of the week, so after gathering her belongings from the break room, she turned toward Mr. Peterson's office to check the schedule he'd posted for the following week to see which days she was working. She was annoyed to find that she was working the next day, but also surprised to see that he'd chosen to schedule her for closing that day as well of the rest of the days of the week rather than opening. It was fine for her, because she hated being up so early during the summer, but she wondered what it was that had warranted this change. Deciding not to look a gift horse in the mouth, she turned to leave.

As she rounded the corner to pass through the store on her way out, she nearly bumped into another mannequin, a female mannequin dressed in dark blue capris and a sunny yellow tank top. Her bright outfit and silky chestnut hair should have given a welcoming feeling, but her unexpected appearance coupled with the grim look on her face as well as her outstretched fingers that scraped along Carrie's arm as she flailed back all filled her with dread. She briefly thought about calling Mr. Peterson again but swallowed the impulse. He'd already made it clear that he didn't believe or care. If he didn't believe in a group of them getting moved into the break room, then he wouldn't believe about one moved slightly away from her position in the store, though it was significantly more than slightly, Carrie realized. Young women's clothing was up by the front, not the back, since their primary customers were women.

Carrie gripped the handle of her lunch box tightly in her hand. Working the closing shift was going to be a lot less fun with these creepy things all around the store in the dark with her. But she wasn't going to let whoever was bullying her drive her away from this job. Instead, she pushed her way past the mannequin, not noticing how it seemed to turn with her as she bumped into it lightly on her way past. She wouldn't entertain it any longer. She was off the clock, so it was someone else's responsibility to get it back to its spot.

~~~

When Carrie arrived for her first time running the closing shift, she felt refreshed from a good night's sleep and excited for working into the evening. She checked her watch. Five more hours of allowing customers inside, then another thirty minutes for her to wrap up getting the store settled down for the night. She tried to surreptitiously ask her coworkers if anything had been going on with the mannequins during the day. They all gave her odd looks like she was crazy, so she quickly stopped asking. From the little bit that she'd asked, though, it sounded like nothing had happened. Which was honestly even more frustrating. *Why* was she the only one being targeted? It wasn't fair!

Before she knew it, she was alone, so she locked the front door, turned down the lights, and got to work getting everything settled for the evening. As she worked, she kept thinking she saw movement in her peripheral vision. Every time she looked up, though, there was nothing there. Well, a couple of times there were mannequins, but not near her. They were always where they were supposed to be. Feeling slightly uneasy, she tried to stay busy and put it out of her mind. But then she started thinking she was hearing things. Slight shuffling sounds, and...possibly even faint whispers? Had she just heard her name?

"Carrie, come here, please!"

Carrie jumped violently and turned toward the sound, and

then she breathed a sigh of relief as she recognized the voice she had heard. Mr. Peterson. That's right, he was still there. Before she could reply, though, something curled around her waist. She looked down to see a mannequin arm bent awkwardly around her. She looked back up and behind her to see that female mannequin from before holding her. The mannequin's whole face seemed to have shifted, eyes alarmingly wide and mouth twisted into some kind of horrible grimace. That shouldn't be possible! She gave a faint cry of terror before bellowing, "Mr. Peterson! Mr. Peterson, help me!"

"Carrie?" he asked. He started to walk around the corner and hesitated when he saw her with the mannequin.

Impossibly, then, the mannequin began to turn, tugging her along with its arm, which would not budge no matter how hard she pushed at it. It pulled her away from Mr. Peterson. "No! Let me go! Help, please!"

Her cries finally snapped Mr. Peterson out of his daze, and he charged forward. Before he could gain much ground, more mannequins came to life, moving to intercept him. Two male mannequins, another female, and the little girl mannequin shuffled jerkily into his path, arms raised and fingers splayed menacingly like claws. He gave a garbled cry as they surrounded him, clawing at his clothes. He struggled fiercely, trying to free himself. He managed to kick the little girl mannequin in the head, sending her reeling away, her head knocked loose from her body. She laid where she'd landed, unmoving.

The mannequin holding Carrie was persistent, clinging tightly and continuously dragging Carrie no matter how hard she struggled. What was going on? How could this be happening? How were some of these mannequins coming to life? *Where was it taking her?* As Mr. Peterson continued to yell and flail against those attacking him, Carrie finally realized the direction the mannequin was taking her: toward the front door. *What?* Was it planning to take her somewhere? Or just trying to make her leave?

She heard a triumphant yell from Mr. Peterson and looked up to see two more mannequins lying at his feet and him grappling with the last one. He ripped one of its arms off and swung it like a bat repeatedly until he knocked the mannequin's head loose. He panted heavily, his eyes wild and crazy looking. A warning shivered through Carrie, then, and suddenly she was glad she was so close to the front door; she wasn't sure she wanted to be near him when he looked like that.

He looked at her then, a strange grin still on his face. "Don't worry, Carrie," he said. "I'll save you."

He moved forward purposefully, tossing aside the mannequin arm as he went. She was surprised, wondering why he threw aside his weapon until he reached inside his suit jacket and pulled out a handgun. The mannequin's movements grew more pronounced, yet also jerkier as it pushed her more forcefully for the door. Was it…was it trying to protect her?

"That's quite enough of that," Mr. Peterson said in a cold voice. Then the sound of gunfire rang out, and Carrie screamed as the mannequin's head above her exploded. Its arm fell from her waist, releasing her as it fell to the ground.

Carrie looked up from the broken mannequin to see Mr. Peterson watching her. "Um…" she began, very unsettled, "thank you. I'm…I'm going to go home now." She fumbled for the door lock, trying to get it free so that she could run outside, but she felt a hand clasp around her wrist.

Mr. Peterson grinned and leaned forward. "Oh, I'm afraid I can't allow that," he said in a falsely cheery voice. He put the gun down on a nearby display table and then pulled out a handkerchief. He pressed it to her face, and try as she might, she couldn't pull away from it. It was wet and smelled sickly sweet, and her head immediately began to swim. As her legs gave out, he lowered her to the floor, and he caressed her face. "You're so pretty," he crooned. "You'll make a wonderful addition to my collection." Then she faded away, her heart seizing with fear.

~~~

Carrie slowly awoke, her mind fuzzy. She couldn't remember where she was or what she had been doing. Panic started clearing the cobwebs from her mind as she realized that she couldn't move. She tried to scream, but no sound would come out, like she was trapped in some kind of horrid nightmare. She heard movement around her, and though she didn't exactly open her eyes, suddenly she could see. It was very bright, and slowly she was able to take in her surroundings. She was in the department store. In the distance, she could see one of her coworkers going around and straightening the folded clothes on the tables. She cast a couple of surreptitious looks over at Carrie, but otherwise kept quiet and away, focused on her work.

What was going on? Why was she in the store? Why was her coworker ignoring her? What— The feeling of hands running down her sides as a shirt was pulled over her head startled her, and she would have jumped with a shiver rolling through her body if she had been able to move. Someone passed into her line of sight, their hands trailing along her figure as they fussed over the clothing they were putting on her. She was shocked to see that it was Mr. Peterson. He hummed lightly as he worked, then smiled at her as he looked up at her face. Glancing over his shoulder to be sure his employee was far away, he whispered, "I was right. You are a lovely addition." Then he lifted her by the waist, carrying her until he got her positioned where he wanted her.

He left then. She still couldn't move at all, but just within her line of sight to her left was another mannequin who was turned to face her. She felt like she could see everything now, the anguish and fear and desperation in their eyes. She wanted to move, to run, to scream, to cry. But she could do nothing, trapped in some kind of prison that she didn't fully understand. The only thing she did know was that it was too late to matter.

Identity

Julie sighed heavily as she dragged herself back up into the attic of her parents' old house. Ever the dutiful daughter, she found herself once again called in to help with the latest project her mother had deemed necessary. *"I just can't bear to think how messy that attic has gotten,"* her mother had wearily said one day, glancing out of the corner of her eye at her daughter as she drove her mom to her doctor's visit. Julie had sighed then too and told her mom that she'd come and do some work on it. Her mother never asked her directly to do anything, just dropped "hints" about what she wanted, expecting that her daughter would follow through. Julie didn't mind though…mostly. Sometimes, she would get frustrated, but it was an odd sensation, almost as though another presence deep within her mind railed at the obligatory filial duty. She just chalked it up to stress.

She made it back into the attic again and took stock of the situation. After several hours of work, everything had been pretty well organized, and she was down to one more small box. Written on the top of the box were the words "home movies," and upon opening the box, Julie found a pile of unlabeled video cassettes. She frowned as she sifted through them. In all her 25 years, she'd never seen any of these. Weren't home movies the sort of thing families watched semi-regularly? She knew her friend Amy's family broke out the family videos for things like birthdays and anniversaries. How old must these tapes be if she didn't even remember them being recorded? Her first instinct was to ask her mother about them, but a niggling feeling in the back of her mind told her not to. She was unused to such a suspicious feeling, but she couldn't deny that her gut told her that her parents would lie if she mentioned the tapes. So she gathered the box in her arms and crept back down the attic stairs, before quietly tiptoeing through the house to the front door to get the box out of sight as quickly as possible.

"Julie?" her mom called as she heard the squeak of the screen door.

Julie quickly sat the box on the stoop just outside the door frame and spun around quickly, letting the door shut again behind her. "Yeah, Mom?" she asked as her mom poked her head into the hallway from the kitchen.

"What are you doing?" her mom asked.

"Yeah, you're not leaving already, are you?" her father called from the living room.

"Oh, I was just letting out a fly that somehow got in," Julie said awkwardly. "But I do think I'll go soon. I'm pretty grimy from crawling around the dusty attic," she added.

Her dad just grunted from his chair in the living room, but her mom pursed her lips slightly. "Well, you needn't have bothered if it were going to be such an inconvenience," she sniffed.

Julie withheld a sigh and forced a smile to her face. "I didn't mean it like that, Mom," she said, trying to placate her. "I'm just worn out. I'd like to go home and get a shower and just relax before work tomorrow."

"Well," her mom said, looking away, "you can go home after

you've had dinner. Now go wash up and set the table."

Julie clenched her jaw, wishing she could just leave, but she knew she couldn't. She was just so anxious to see what was on those video tapes. Still, she did as she was told, going to wash her hands and the worst of the grime from her face in the bathroom before getting the table set to eat with her parents.

~~~

After finally making it home, weary from the long day of working and the hour-long drive home, Julie went straight to her living room with the box of VHS tapes to start exploring them. She was smugly pleased that she had kept the VHS player all these years despite disparaging remarks from others that it was too obsolete and couldn't be worth the space it took on her TV stand anymore. Moments like this were exactly why she'd kept it. She frowned again as she pulled out a tape, displeased that there were no labels on them to help her know in advance what was on each. She popped the tape in the player, then got up to grab some masking tape and a permanent marker so that she could label them herself as she viewed them.

The first one turned out to be quite old. She could tell from her parents' appearances that it was made before she'd even been born, and she felt a stab of disappointment. She wondered if all of these tapes were going to end up being this old. She'd been interested in seeing some footage taken during her childhood. Her early memory was oddly sparse, leaving her unable to remember much before the age of six or seven. Julie knew that was odd, had been told that often enough throughout her life, and it bothered her more than she let on to others. She was curious to see if any recorded memories could help spark organic memories in her mind.

With a sigh, she picked up the remote and started fast-forwarding through the tape, uninterested in watching her parents on their vacation to Texas that they'd taken early in their relationship. She watched the blurred images flash by, showing her parents—mostly her mom, as her dad apparently wielded the camera most often—go from city to city and landmark to landmark, smiling and laughing and apparently having a grand old time. She watched the image wistfully, keenly aware of how different they seemed here from most of her experience. They'd never been so fun or joyful for much of her memory. Julie felt a stab of resentment as the tape snapped to a halt, reaching the end of its content; it almost seemed as if bringing her into the world had made them the clinical, brisk people she knew, and she couldn't help but feel angry at the thought. She tried to push that feeling aside as she dutifully rewound the tape before removing it from the player, knowing that she couldn't really know when or why their personalities changed. The feeling still persisted, however, lightly within her chest, unwilling to be silenced. She meticulously labeled the tape "Texas Vacation" before moving to grab the next one.

The next tape was another early one; it held footage from her parents' wedding. She didn't know who was operating the camera this time, but it was obviously neither of her parents since they were always the objects of the frames. She watched her father stand up at the front of the aisle with his groomsmen at his side and the bridesmaids on the other, all of them gathered beneath a natural awning of trees at the outdoor wedding. Julie sat enraptured as her mother and her grandfather started coming down the aisle. When her mother reached the front to stand opposite her father and turned so that she was almost facing the cameraman, Julie was shocked to see a distinct baby bump. Her mother was pregnant when she and her father got married? They'd never told her that before. As much as they'd lectured her about the importance of staying chaste until marriage, it had never once occurred to her that they themselves hadn't practiced what they'd preached. She couldn't help a derisive snort. Figured. Was her mom pregnant with her? She tried to quickly do that math but couldn't quite remember what year her parents had gotten married. Still, she must have been, because Julie didn't have any siblings.

Before long, the wedding ceremony ended, and the wedding party disappeared for photos. While they were gone, the cameraman went around to various individuals in the crowd, collecting well wishes for the newlywed couple. Julie listened idly, not caring much for what these people had to say. But just when she was about to start fast-forwarding again, the current person's words stopped her cold.

"And we're just *so* excited to see the little ones when they arrive!"

Little ones? Julie thought confused. They were expecting more than one child? She listened a little longer, but no one else seemed interested in talking about the pregnancy, and Julie finally got impatient and started fast-forwarding again, hoping the tape would switch to a future date after her mother had given birth, but the tape screeched to a halt again.

Frustrated, Julie ripped the tape from the VCR, stopping just long enough to use the tape and marker to label it "Wedding. Pregnant??" before popping in the next tape. The next one was older, showing more vacation footage, and Julie wanted to scream in frustration. She didn't give a damn about their early life travels; she wanted to know what that person was talking about! She fast-forwarded through the whole tape just in case, and when nothing came of it, she pulled the tape and tossed it aside, not bothering with a label.

With the next tape, though, she finally struck gold. The tape started right away showing two infants, both in matching onesies that only differed by the names lovingly embroidered on the chests: Julie and Jenny. Julie watched slack-jawed as the two babies cooed and kicked their feet in the air, delighting at their mother and father hovering above them and showering them with love. She was dumbstruck. Julie must be her... but who on earth was Jenny? She didn't have a sister; she'd never had a sister...had she? Her head started hurting, and she clutched at her temple. She wished so fiercely to remember, but nothing would come to mind. But her chest felt tight with an amalgamation of feelings she couldn't identify.

Surprisingly, the dominant feeling that surged to the surface was uncharacteristic rage. Lies. Her life was all *lies*. Her parents had lied to her. Deceived her. She clenched her hand against her chest as if to repress the feelings that threatened to burst forth from her chest. Leaping to her feet, she slapped the stop button on the VCR and then spun to grab her phone, furiously dialing her parents' phone number. She worried her jaw while waiting for them to pick up. Finally, her mother answered.

"Hello?"

"Who is Jenny?" Julie demanded, not bothering to say hello first. There was a pause, too long to be anything but suspicious.

"Where did you hear that name?"

Julie ground her teeth. "There was a box of old videos up in your attic. Forgot you left them up there? I've been watching them. When were you going to tell me I had a sister once? And *why* didn't you tell me?!" she shouted into the receiver.

"Julie, you mustn't watch any more of those videos!" her mother said in a panicked voice.

Julie felt a wave of guilt that she'd upset her mom, but she rallied past it. "Tell me the truth, then!" Julie yelled. "Either you tell me, or these tapes will!"

"Julie, please!"

There were muffled sounds on the other side of the phone, followed by a muffled exchange between her parents: "She found the tapes. She knows about Jenny." "What?! Why didn't you throw those away?"

There was more commotion on the other end of the line, and then it was her father speaking to her. "Julie, you listen to me," he said sternly. "You put those tapes down and leave them alone. We're coming over right now to talk!" He hung up the phone.

Julie threw her phone to the side, fighting the urge to comply with his command, instead rushing to be sure her doors and windows were all locked. She knew better, all trust and good faith in her parents gone. They weren't coming to give her answers. They were coming to take away the tapes and leave her in the dark. But she wouldn't allow that! She had one hour before they arrived, one hour to find the truth for herself!

She pushed the play button again, but there was nothing else recorded on the tape, so she ripped it from the player and tried another. The next couple were both older, once again showing footage from vacations her parents took together. "Ugh, what narcissistic jerks!" she muttered, pulling the second tape from the player in frustration. She was running out of time! She needed to know. It felt like the truth was right there on the edge of her mind, just begging to be known if only the right key would come to unlock the memory.

She pressed in a third tape, and this time was rewarded with more footage of two identical little girls. They were older now, probably around four or five years old. Once again, they were dressed in identical clothing—little pink and white jumpsuits with pale pink undershirts and little white tennis shoes—and once again their names were embroidered on the front of their clothes: Julie and Jenny. *Of course Mom would choose a ridiculous style like stitching our names to our shirts,* she thought with an eyeroll, but at least it helped her now to know which was herself and which was her sister. The two girls gamboled around together, talking to one another quietly, playing some game that apparently only the two of them understood. In the audio track, she could hear her mother giggling as she watched, calling to the little girls. "Julie, Jenny! Look over here girls!" The camera tilted to a skewed angle as her father's voice faintly appeared, calling the mother away for something. "Be right there, dear!" The camera leveled out again as her mother sat it down on some type of surface. "I'll be back in a minute, girls. Don't get up to too many shenanigans!"

She left the room, and all that remained were the two little girls. Julie watched as Jenny reached out and pulled little Julie's hair, making her cry. In retaliation, Julie pushed Jenny away, knocking her down, and a dark expression crossed Jenny's face. She pushed herself back up and looked around. Then she walked away to a nearby table to pick something up, then walked back to Julie. She raised her hand, and the Julie watching the tape squinted, trying to tell what Jenny was holding. Her eyes widened as she recognized a letter opener. Moments later, Jenny grabbed Julie and thrust the pointy letter opener into her throat. Julie screamed a loud, garbled scream and fell back. Jenny dropped onto her and plunged the letter opener into her throat and face again and again, not making a sound, just glaring that exceptionally frightening expression as she stabbed her sister repeatedly. Finally, Jenny laid the letter opener aside and stood up. Her clothes were awash with blood as were Julie's. Julie didn't get up; she laid unmoving on the floor, her chest not lifting, not breathing. "Okay, girls, what do we want to—" A piercing wail rang out, and her mother rushed into the frame and fell to her knees beside Julie. "Noooo! Julie! What happened?!" Her father rushed into the room next, shock apparent on his face too. They both looked at each other, then cast terrified expressions at Jenny who stood calmly watching both of them, no emotion on her face. The tape ended.

Julie stared at the TV static in shock. How could she have survived such an attack? She hadn't looked alive at all in the video. And she...she didn't have any scars on her neck or face. She lurched over to a decorative mirror that hung in her living room to look and be sure she wasn't crazy. No scars at all. So how...how did any of what she saw make sense? Jenny had just....

Jenny.

She was *Jenny. She* had killed her sister. That was the only explanation. But then...why did she think she was Julie? What had her parents done to her?

She checked her watch. Twenty minutes. Just enough time to check another tape or two. She started another tape and was relieved to see that it seemed to have more information. In the footage, she sat in a chair at the back of a room, staring blankly at three adults who sat in a room before her. Two of them were her parents, and the third appeared to be a doctor, a man wearing a white lab coat. "I just want to be quite clear on what you're looking for here, why you came to me instead of the authorities," the doctor said.

Jenny's mother crossed her arms, her face a mixture of grief and rage. "She murdered our daughter, our sweet darling Julie!"

"Yes, I'm aware of that," the doctor replied, sounding bored. "So why haven't you called the authorities to report the death?"

Jenny's father spoke up. "If we report what happened, they'll lock Jenny away, and we won't have any children. We want Julie back."

The doctor raised an eyebrow. "Surely you know that resurrection is impossible."

"We're not idiots," her mother snapped. "We came to you because we know what kind of work you do, what kind of research you conduct. And we know you've been researching some...alternative treatments and goals." She jerked her head at her daughter. "So make her be Julie. Make her be the daughter we should have had, the daughter that she *owes* us."

The doctor leaned forward, rubbing his chin thoughtfully. "Full personality adjustment," he murmured. "Suppress one and create another. It's certainly...intriguing."

"Then you'll do it?" Jenny's father asked.

The doctor nodded. "I'll try."

The footage ended for a moment, then resumed in a different room. Jenny was struggling, strapped into a chair, her hair shaved off and electrodes and wires connected all over her body, especially her head. "Your name is Julie!" the doctor's voice stated.

Jenny shook her head. "No, I'm Jenny!" She screamed before convulsing as a jolt of electricity shot through her.

"There is no Jenny! There never was a Jenny! You are Julie!"

This continued for a short while, Jenny trying to resist before finally whimpering, "I'm Julie."

But that wasn't enough. The doctor continued. "Julie is a

sweet, obedient little girl. She obeys her parents!"

"J-Julie...she's..." Jenny screamed again as the electricity coursed through her again.

The footage continued, but Jenny finally shut it off after a short while, too shaken to keep watching it. She knew the ending anyhow. They had succeeded. They'd made her docile, made her become Julie. Rage burned within her again, and for once, instead of feeling foreign and frightening, it felt *right*. They had tortured her! They had taken her identity from her! They would *pay*. Her expression went very calm as she heard a car pull up outside. It was time. She walked gracefully into the kitchen, out of sight of the living room, and waited for them to let themselves in with the key she'd given them, the key they had *made* her give to them.

"Julie!" her mother called in a wobbly voice.

"Julie, where are you?" her father boomed. He walked toward the bathroom looking for her while her mother went into the living room.

"I found the tapes!" her mother hollered. "She must be here somewhere! Help me get these!"

Her father started to walk into the living room too, but Jenny walked up behind him, firmly planting a hand on his shoulder to spin him around. "Jul—" he gasped, air abandoning his lungs as she plunged a butcher's knife deep into his chest. She smiled serenely at him, then pulled the knife back out to slash his throat. She passed through the shower of blood and stepped over him to advance on her mother who cowered, screaming, on the floor of the living room, huddling amongst the tapes that contained all the damning evidence.

"Julie, please!" she begged.

"My name is Jenny."

"J-Jenny, honey, I'm sorry. Please, can't we just talk?"

Jenny continued her advance. "What is there to talk about? Do you want to explain why you didn't love me? Why did Julie deserve your love but I didn't?"

Jenny's mother's face turned vicious. "You *killed* Julie! What were we supposed to do, give you a gold star and a lollipop? You killed our baby!"

Jenny glowered in return. "*I* was your baby too!" She sprang forward and tackled her mother, plunging the blade into her chest. "I was your baby! I was! You should have loved me too! Why didn't you love me! This is your fault! It's your fault! YOUR FAULT!" She screamed and screamed, losing herself to her fury and the knife plunged up and down like a needle on a sewing machine. Finally she stopped and came back to herself, taking in the veritable sea of blood spreading across the floor of her living room. Her mother's corpse lay beneath her, nearly unrecognizable now from the stab wounds to the torso and face.

Jenny stood and calmly walked back into the kitchen, tenderly wiping the butcher's knife clean before setting it reverently on the table. After she got cleaned up, it would come with her. She wasn't sure yet where she was going, but the future was wide-open before her. She had her identity back, and she'd dealt with the evils of the past. She'd been wronged, but she had corrected it. And with that knife, that beautiful knife, she would always be able to ensure that she was treated properly in the future.

About the Author

T. M. Delaney is a writer of novels and short stories. They live in Missouri with their cat Remy, their official creative "mews." T. M. Delaney spent several years working in publishing before changing to a career in graphic design. In their spare time, they love listening to music, reading, playing video games, and spending time with friends and family.

T. M. Delaney most commonly writes m/m romance novels, but also has plans for non-romance titles as well. Their interests are wide, including urban fantasy, magical realism, paranormal, and realistic fiction to name a few. Angst and comfort are their specialties, as is mixing spicy heat with tender sweetness.

Want to connect with this author? Check out their author newsletter at tmdelaney.substack.com for regular updates about their life, their writing projects, upcoming titles, and adorable pictures of their cat.

Subscribe to my newsletter:
✉ https://tmdelaney.substack.com

Also by T. M. Delaney

Eerie: A Collection of 10 Chilling Tales
A collection of 10 chilling tales of horror. What would you do if your neighbors were stalking you? What if your reflection started moving on its own? What if your dead daughter called you from the grave? What consequences might befall those who only know how to follow? Or rebellious youths who pry where they shouldn't? Delve into these tales if you dare.

Get your copy today: https://books2read.com/Eerie-A-Collection-of-10-Chilling-Tales

www.ingramcontent.com/pod-product-compliance
Lightning Source LLC
LaVergne TN
LVHW092055060526
838201LV00047B/1403